CRIMEUCOPIA

The Lady Thrillers
A Murderous Ink Press Anthology

****

CRIMEUCOPIA

The Lady Thrillers

First published by
Murderous-Ink Press
Crowland
LINCOLNSHIRE
England
www.murderousinkpress.co.uk

Acknowledgements

To those writers and artists who helped make this anthology what it is, I can only say a heartfelt Thank You!

And to Den, as always.

Contents

*Taken from *The Black Widow Club: Nine Tales of Obsession and Murder* (2013)

CANADIAN AUTHORS

Vivian Heather

Leesa JoAnn Iverson

Gail Lowe

Olyn Ozbick

Meghan Victoria

L.K. Weir

https://thecornerlotauthors.com/

The Lipstick On His Collar Doesn't Seem To Match Mine….
(An Editorial of Sorts)

As most authors will tell you, when you start out writing fiction there will come a time when someone will dust off and decant that old adage which goes:

'Always write about what you know.'

Oh dear.

Another adage is that 'Little girls are made of sugar and spice and all things nice.'

Oh dear, oh dear, oh dear. What does all that say about the women authors contained within these pages?

Originally Jack and I thought that material for this volume would be slow in arriving. That it would be one of those 'forever back burner' projects that wouldn't see the light of print until x-many 'whatevers' down the publishing line.

How wrong we were. And how gratifying it was to be proven wrong, especially when we were told in a discussion forum, in no uncertain terms, that the day of the short story was long gone – a victim of flash fiction and the CV-19 novel writing boom.

There are still people who want something to read – be it

paper or electronic – that is short, sharp and satisfying – before immersing themselves in their next novel. Flash Fiction has its rightful place, but sometimes it's nice to have a little more flesh on those shallow grave bones.

So, contained in this collection are, in no particular order:-

Karen Skinner, who introduces her female Private Investigator, Liz Philips, in the first of a series of ten shorts.

Lena Ng brings a possible murder to the table, while Ginny Swart takes us to the Southern hemisphere with deceptively casual writing style, even though the setting is very modern.

Kate Miller and Sandrine Bergès both give us period pieces set in France, but in completely different centuries, while Linda Kerr steps away from her Nellie Fearon persona and enters the Crime side.

Hilary Davidson, when not writing bestselling novels, tells of a club that sounds all too real for our liking, and Kelly Lewis presents a pet shop with a difference.

Michelle Ann King presents a humorous, albeit modern-NOIR style, and keeping on the darker side of humour, Paulene Turner tells the tale of a more than slightly tarnished bodyguard.

Tiffany Lindfield's offering has a foundation that although we may believe we have free will and choice, Astrology feels that we can only play the cards we're dealt, and the outcome is always predestined.

Claire Leng takes us headlong into the 21st Century, and adds that the acronym WIFU is a slang for a fictional female character that people obsess too much over.

Madeleine McDonald gives us a curious spin on traditions

and moral values, as does Pauline Gostling, who provides another kind of dilemma that is perhaps more relevant today than in the past. And Amanda Steel deftly opens the box marked 'When is a crime not a crime?'

And to close out this first anthology, Joan Hall Hovey presents a powerful tale, salted here and there with just a touch of dark humour.

Hopefully you will find something that you immediately like – or, in the spirit of the Murderous Ink Press motto – "You never know what you like until you read it."

Pretty Wicked
Karen Skinner

In my experience, those who beg for mercy seldom deserve it. In fact, it's really an admission of guilt. They're saying, '*Yes, I did it, but I didn't want to get caught. How do I get out of this?*'

The answer is up to you. I personally found this shift in power hugely satisfying. You now have the option to choose. Do you let them go, or do you give them what you know they deserve?

I'd never held a ceremonial sword before. It was a lot heavier than I expected, but I managed to balance it by letting it rest against the hollow at the base of his throat. As he lay there on his back with anxious eyes pleading, I couldn't help thinking that he looked like a desperate starfish; caught out of water with his arms and legs askew. I chuckled at the image in my mind and he started to beg again.

*****

My original office was in Templeton Street in a leafy Hertfordshire town. The building had an accountant above, a solicitor below and me, Elizabeth Philips Investigations, in the middle. Now, the brass plate that I'd polished every week is a coaster for my new desk – my dining table at home. In reality I found I couldn't afford the business rates on my own.

I've been running *EPI* for about 10 years, so when my apprentice PI, Danny Johnson, came into my old office that morning and dropped the buff coloured file onto my desk, like he had hundreds of others, I only glanced at it and pretended not to be excited.

"It's another missing girl, Liz," he said with all the pent up adrenaline of a small boy looking forward to a promised treat.

"Uh huh." I carried on typing.

"That makes four."

"Hmmm."

Danny sat on the edge of my desk and creased the edges of my unfiled reports. I gave him a stern but typical-of-you look and he obligingly lifted a buttock to let me retrieve them.

"Aww, c'mon Liz," he cajoled. "Don't tell me this isn't getting you going. I know you too well. You always get stoked over a new case. I know I do."

I squinted at the computer screen and deleted a line of text.

"Well, go shake hands with yourself in the loo, then. I'm busy."

Danny sighed and slid off the desk. I couldn't help but watch him go as he made his way to the outer office. God, he was hot. Too bad he had a philanderer's reputation. He'd flirt with the office pot plant if he thought he'd get anywhere.

I knew that within ten minutes he'd be on the internet, looking up the other cases and seeing if he could make a connection. That was what I liked about Danny, apart from the dark hair and grey green eyes, of course. Under that flirtatious, ego protective shell was a determined and intelligent personality, capable of making quick deductions. And if he ever met with any resistance, he'd just flirt you into submission. I'd also noticed that his charm worked just as well with men as it did with women. Too bad he couldn't charm the BTEC qualification he needed for his own licence.

I glared at the screen and deleted another line. I was always very particular about writing my reports correctly. If the police ever did want to cut us some slack, they might discover that we could be useful, and proper reports go a long way in presenting a professional image.

I rubbed my hands over my face and tried to remember when I last took a break. The new file winked at me just at the peripheral edge of my vision, beckoning me like a forbidden chocolate bar.

It has always been one of my golden rules to finish one job before moving onto the next. But that was now tarnished to more of a bronze hue. I'd broken that rule more times than even I could remember. Still, a brief flick through couldn't hurt.

The police looked on private investigators like us as if we were a joke. I don't mean that all of them treated us with contempt, just that some did. I knew they thought we were funny; silly kids playing at being grownups. But when they had exhausted all the leads, and frantic relatives were one phone call away from a psychic hotline, that was usually when our phone would ring.

From the cover sheet it looked like the older sister, Rebecca Pierce, had made the call this time. Danny had printed out the photograph she'd kindly emailed over and I identified the missing girl, Jenny, almost immediately. She stood in the middle, between two friends, with her arms around their shoulders, at what looked like a nightclub bar. She had been missing for three weeks.

She was a pretty, dark haired girl. 19 years old, and around 5ft 9 with a charming smile. Just like the other three, she'd failed to return home after a night out. We hadn't had the pleasure of becoming acquainted with the files of the other girls, so similarities could only be guessed at. But Danny, forever Mr Efficiency, had helpfully included relevant newspaper clippings.

I skimmed through Danny's procedural form and as it turned out, all previous boyfriends had been contacted and excluded from enquires. All her friends had been questioned too, but this was where we usually dug a little deeper. We didn't just question friends; we talked to anyone, including enemies and toxic friends; those who were too scared to say too much for fear of suspicion.

There was a toxic friend in the photograph. Older, sexier and worldlier than Jenny, and way too cool to smile for the phone camera. Toxic friends usually hung out with their mates because the good friend had something that the bad friend wanted; a lover, peer status, intelligence, sometimes money.

I studied the photograph again. This toxic friendship was about love. Jenny was loved. She and her good friend smiled openly at the camera, excited to be there. Her toxic friend had obviously been to that venue too many times before to be excited. She leaned in towards Jenny slightly but didn't show any particular emotion.

A quick call to Rebecca had confirmed that she had taken the photograph herself at a local nightclub where Jenny had celebrated her nineteenth birthday. Tickets had been a surprise present from her friend, Emma, who worked there.

I glanced at the clock and sighed. So maybe I could combine a break with a long lunch. I grabbed my coat and shoulder bag from the hook on the back of the door, told Danny I was off out, and jogged down the stairs and on to the street.

*****

My ancient Astra was all I could afford after my divorce. It had upholstery that smelt like fish and chips and a cassette player where a DAB radio ought to be. It reluctantly got me to Birchwood Terrace at a quarter to twelve. As I rang Emma's doorbell, I wondered if I'd be waking her. If she worked at the local nightclub, then I assumed she'd be sleeping.

An unshaven young man in his twenties opened the door. He was wearing a tee shirt and boxers.

"Yeah?"

"Hi, I'm Liz Phillips; I've come to see Emma."

He looked confused for a moment, and then opened the door. He said nothing as I followed him in to a cramped and untidy front room.

"'ad friends over," he said, by way of explanation. He beckoned to a settee and walked out into the hallway to yell up the stairs.

I pushed yesterday's clothes out of the way and sat as close to the edge as I could without falling off.

He took a breath and shouted, "Em!"

An angry, "Wot?" came down from above.

"Bird down 'ere for ya."

It had been a few years since I'd been referred to as a bird. I tried not to smile as I heard him break wind several times then head off into the kitchen.

Emma walked into the living room the way most beautiful women walk into an office. She was wearing a neat blouse and tailored trousers, and her makeup was immaculately applied. She dropped herself elegantly into a nearby chair.

"This'll have to be quick," she said, removing an invisible hair. "Got stock taking to do this afternoon. Cuppa tea?" she offered.

I smiled politely, "Thanks, but no." If this was her living room, I didn't want to know what her kitchen looked like. Clearly her looks were her first priority.

"You want to talk about Jenny," she stated, getting straight to the point.

"Um, yes," I said unable to hide my surprise.

"Your shoes," she said pointing to my sensible flats. "Dead giveaway."

I may only be 5ft 4 and a half, but heels don't go with my jeans-and-shirt uniform.

"So, how long…?"

"Since senior school," she cut in, pre-empting again. "Best mates forever. No, I don't know where she might be, or what other mates she has. We didn't have a row the last time I saw her and no, I don't know of anyone who hated her enough to bump her off."

Her boyfriend came in just then, sat on top of the abandoned clothes next to me and released the ring pull on a can of beer. Emma gave him a look that could have frozen molten lava.

"Hair of the dog, innit?" he said indignantly.

"You could at least have put some clothes on," scolded Emma.

"My 'ouse."

I raised an eyebrow at the boyfriend and he obligingly filled in the details. I've found that if you give people enough space, the need to explain will overpower the need to conceal.

"My dad owns the nightclub and I help out. Met her there." He nodded toward Emma. "Dad owns this place and we get cheap rent."

"Did Jenny ever come here?" I asked.

Suddenly the boyfriend was lost for words. He looked surprised, perhaps not so much by the question, but that it was directed at him.

"Don't 'fink so," he replied, a little too quickly. He stared back at me with wide eyes, but didn't look at Emma. I returned his gaze.

You slept with her, didn't you? But I kept the thought to myself.

"No," said Emma, answering my initial question. "I only moved in with Ben just a week before she disappeared. We hadn't had time to send out house warming invites."

"Daft idea," sniffed Ben, taking a gulp of beer. "Been 'ere ages."

I looked at Emma as she spoke. Her voice remained calm, but her eyes were cold. She knew he'd been unfaithful, but perhaps not with whom.

"Is there a security camera covering the outside gate of the nightclub?" I asked, getting an idea.

Ben took another swig of beer from the can, then asked, "You mean where the car park joins the road? No need. Cameras are all over the inside and over every door, plus a few in the car park. Once they're on the road, they're polices' problem. Why?"

"Well, if we can review the security images we might be able to find out who Jenny partied with, but now might not get to see who she left with."

Ben shrugged. "Police took 'em all away a couple of weeks ago."

I pulled the group photograph from my bag. "Who's the other girl here with you?" I asked Emma.

"That's Maria, a friend of Jen's sister." Emma sniffed disapprovingly. She must have suspected her of being the girl Ben slept with.

I showed the picture to Ben. He looked a little sad when he saw it, but shrugged and shook his head when I pointed to Maria. He didn't know her.

Emma, trying to remember, said, "Her dad is the local mayor, isn't he? She dated a bloke a little while back, but they split up soon after Jen went missing."

I could hear an alarm bell ring quietly in the back of my head.

"Do you know where I can find her?" I asked as casually as I could.

"There's a do on at the town hall tonight. She'll be there." The tone of Emma's voice suggested that she wouldn't be going.

*****

Danny wasn't in the office when I returned but had left me a message saying he was going to talk to Rebecca again. He suspected that she had been having an affair with an ex-boyfriend of Jenny's.

That was an avenue to explore, but my senses were leading me in another direction and so I left him a message on his mobile to dress to impress this evening. We had an event to attend.

*****

I arrived late as usual and a glance at my watch told me that it was far too late to be fashionable.

I wasn't used to wearing high heeled shoes and a proper dress, and judging by the looks I got from the well-to-do ladies already present, it showed.

The local great and good were gathered together in elegant surroundings. Most were there to be congratulated for giving away what they wouldn't miss, to the more popular national charities. At one end, the mayor was already centre stage, thanking everyone for being as wonderful as him, and I immediately tuned him out so I could scan the crowd.

Maria was to the front of the crowd, gazing at her father as if he was a hero. She was wearing a pretty pale blue dress and looked as if she'd had her hair done for the occasion. I took a closer look at the people around her and it appeared that she was unescorted.

I made my way over to her and waited for her father to finish his speech and absorb the applause before I introduced myself to her. Her polite smile faded a little as she shook my hand and I noticed her lips tremble slightly when I mentioned Jenny's name.

Quietly, I asked, "Is there anywhere we can talk more privately?"

She nodded and led me to a side room, closing the door behind us.

We were surrounded by the ornaments of official office. The table pushed against the far wall was stacked with all the regalia removed to make room in the main hall.

Plaster coats of arms fought for space with banners and what seemed like spears adorned with red ropes.

"Look," she began, sounding agitated, "It's only going to be a few minutes before people notice I'm not there."

"This will be really brief, I promise. I only have few questions and I know that they're going to sound strange, but I'd really appreciate it if you could be honest with me, ok?"

She nodded. "Ok."

"First of all, can you tell me how old you are?"

Maria looked a little surprised, but I'd already rumbled her. There was no need to pretend.

"I'm fifteen," she admitted.

I nodded, now understanding. An excellent education and an intelligent mind made peers her own age seem immature, but partying at the places her friends went to made a little subversion necessary. The right clothes and makeup, and a mature attitude would make her appear older than her years. At a nightclub she'd be more likely to meet an older, more appealing man, one she'd be reluctant to invite to an evening like this where her father would meet him.

"What was it that Jenny didn't like about your ex-boyfriend?"

Again Maria raised her eyebrows, but answered the question. "She said he was a user. He only wanted to get me into bed and wouldn't be able to stay faithful."

"Did she say why she thought so?"

"No."

"It's not Ben, is it?" I asked, needing confirmation.

Maria wrinkled her nose. "God, no; I don't know what Emma sees in him."

With his own place and a rich daddy, it wasn't too hard for me to see what Emma saw in him.

Maria looked at me. "Do you know what's happened to Jenny?"

I nodded slowly. "Yes, I think I do. I think that the guy you dated, dated her first and she thought that she should warn you. Did you ever stop to think about how alike the two of you looked; both pretty, petit and dark haired?"

Maria shook her head sadly. "No, I never thought about it."

"I think her boyfriend was attracted to you when he found out who your father was. The other girls in the newspapers were pretty and dark haired, too. And I think that Jenny got in the way when she told him to back off and leave you alone."

Maria looked like she was going to cry and put a hand over her mouth to stifle a sob.

"Did your ex ever know your real age?"

She shook her head again. "I never told him."

This told me all I needed to know and I thanked her as I opened the door for her. I waited in the room a little longer. If my suspicions were correct, the ex-boyfriend would have come here tonight not wanting to miss the opportunity to talk to her father. If he had seen her enter this room with me he'd want to know what we had talked about.

I leant against the table with my arms folded and waited for my visitor. It wasn't long before the door opened slightly and a handsome, cheerful face peeked round to look at me.

"Hi," he said. "Have you had a glass of champagne yet? You'd better be quick; the vultures are eating and drinking everything."

"I can wait," I did my best to sound casual. "Come on in. We need to talk."

He strolled into the middle of the room and let the door close behind him. He stood with his hands in his pockets and shrugged.

"So, what were you two girls gossiping about?" His smile looked forced and unnatural. "Which one of the men out there is the best looking?"

"We were talking about Jenny Pierce," I said calmly. "And who dated her before Maria."

His face paled. "I've heard that Maria has a jealous streak and a mean temper. You should talk to her friends if you think she dated the same man as Jenny."

I couldn't believe he was trying to slander an innocent girl. I raised a wagging finger as I pointed out the telling detail.

"Well, now it's interesting that you just said 'man'. You see, we've always referred to Jenny and her friends as girls, but Jenny wasn't the youngest."

"No?"

"No. Maria is fifteen. So if he dated both girls," I turned my palms towards the ceiling in an open shrug, "With Maria, he'd have been a bit of a bad boy now, wouldn't he?"

I saw him swallow.

"And that would explain why Jenny intervened."

"Well, if she was so concerned about her friend," he responded, sounding anxious, "Why would she bring Maria to a nightclub where everyone is supposed to be over eighteen?"

I wagged my finger again. "There you are with another interesting word, supposed. Not everyone who gets into a nightclub is over eighteen. All you have to do is check out the young faces on the dance floor and who looks too nervous to approach the bar."

I took a short step forward, and looked him directly in the eyes. He had the gall to stare straight back.

"Is that where you met the other girls, Danny? In the nightclubs? Because that seems to be the kind you go for. Pretty, petit, dark haired and young. You'd have a dance with them, invite them out for a nightcap and meet up later in the car park, where the security cameras can't see."

Danny simply smiled. "All you have is a suspicion, a hunch. No hard evidence at all."

"Not if Maria tells us you slept with her."

"A misdemeanour at best," he said dismissively. "She never told me her real age and I believed she was over the age of consent."

"Not if you slept with Jenny, too. That's a direct connection. You see, if a man is smart enough to use a condom, he tends to stick with the brand he likes. Once they find Jenny–" I immediately corrected myself, "When they find Jenny, they'll be able to test for traces of spermicide to tell which brand it was, and compare it with what Maria knows."

I didn't even know if such a test was possible. I was bluffing, but would it be enough?

Danny suddenly lunged forward and put both his hands around my throat. I squealed with shock, but couldn't scream as he squeezed even tighter.

I fumbled behind me and lashed out, smashing a gilded plaque over the top of his head. The plaque flew across the room and Danny staggered backwards on to the floor. Without stopping to think, I reached behind for another weapon and didn't realise I had hold of a ceremonial sword until I heard the blade chink on the floor as it bounced.

I reached down and had to use both hands to hold it up as I pointed the tip of the blade at Danny's throat. He gave a nervous little laugh as he tried to shuffle backwards.

"Where is she, Danny?" I took a step forward and balanced the tip in the hollow under his chin, feeling his Adam's apple push against it as he swallowed. "Where is Jenny?"

I was standing almost right over him now.

"Please, for God's sake, Liz. Please don't do this."

"Tell me where she is."

"Liz, please don't. Please Liz."

I tilted my right hand so that my wrist was pointing towards the ceiling and gently pressed the heel of my left hand against the butt of the decorative handle. I couldn't help admiring how beautiful it was. How balanced.

"You have until I count to five to tell me what you did with Jenny Pierce. One…."

"Oh dear God."

"Two, Three…."

"Liz, I swear to God, I'll tell you everything you want to know. Please put down the sword. Please Liz."

"Four,"

"Liz! Please!"

Suddenly, there was a knock on the door. It was Maria.

"Liz, are you alright in there?" she called.

The Black Widow Club
Hilary Davidson

Oscar looked exactly as he had the last time I'd seen him, except for the chunk missing from the back of his skull. His body was slumped face down on his desk, right hand resting on the computer's mouse, the monogrammed gold cufflinks his company had presented him upon his retirement gleaming in the fluorescent light of the basement. His shirt and chinos were neatly pressed, and his feet were tucked into black suede loafers. What was new was the computer screen splattered with blood and splotches of grey matter that I didn't want to get close enough to analyze.

I forced my eyes away from the corpse. "Mom, when you told me on the phone that *something* had happened to Oscar, was this what you meant?"

My mother's face was wide-eyed in shock. She wore a long silk robe, her pedicured toes peeking out, under the hem, from glittery silver mules. Her mouth trembled but she didn't answer me.

"Have you called the police?" It had taken me ninety minutes of demonic driving to get to her house in Toronto from mine in St. Thomas, Ontario. I'd expected to find an ambulance in the driveway. Instead, my mother met me at the door, wordlessly wringing her hands. I guessed that was what she'd done since calling me around midnight.

"Mom!" I shouted, trying to snap her out of her silence. "Who shot Oscar?"

My mother bit her lower lip. "Let's go to the kitchen, Claire." She turned and clipped up the basement stairs. I took a last look at Oscar and followed her.

"I wouldn't mind a drink, truth be told," she said, puttering around the kitchen. "But that would make me a very bad host because you can't have one. How are you feeling, dear?"

"Fine." I was six months pregnant and long past morning sickness.

"How is my sweet Maddie? I hope I didn't wake her up when I called you."

"She's sleeping over at a friend's house tonight." Which was lucky, I almost added. When I'd left the house at twelve-fifteen, my husband still hadn't come home.

"Oh, a pajama party. How exciting!" My mother set a pink teacup in front of me. "The kettle will boil in a minute."

"Cut it out, Mom. Tell me what happened with Oscar."

"Well, it's difficult to describe, dear. I mean, it will sound silly to you." Her lips quivered. "Oscar has been so… difficult. Ever since he retired. No, that's not true. Ever since I *married* him. But especially since he retired."

My stepfather had left his job as an advertising executive a few months before. He'd often claimed that working on ad campaigns for "retarded sheep" had made him a misanthrope.

"I know he's difficult, Mom. He always has been." I'd never

liked my stepfather. My mother had married him a decade ago, while I was in college. Outside the house, he was the slick, smooth-talking exec known for his sharp style and razor wit. But at home, he was a foul-mouthed bully. At family dinners, I'd tolerated Oscar's politically incorrect outbursts on everything from North Korea (*Truman was a pussy for not nuking them to blazes*) to global warming (*I'm not giving up my SUV for some fucking squirrel in a rainforest*). It was harder to watch him curse out my mother for forgetting to put salt on the dinner table. I'd often wondered how she put up with him. Obviously, she'd hit her breaking point.

"He's been doing everything possible to break my nerves since he retired." My mother poured boiling water into our cups. Her hand trembled, but she didn't spill a drop. "First he started meddling with little things, telling me that I spent too much money on groceries. Then he took back some of the presents I bought for Maddie's birthday. He said I was extravagant. What grandmother isn't?"

I remembered Maddie's sixth birthday party. My mother had arrived with unwrapped presents she had just bought at the local Toys-R-Us. It was out of character for her — she planned ahead, and her gifts were trimmed with ribbons and bows — but she hadn't explained it at the time.

"There have been so many things, Claire. He's been absolute hell to live with. But I haven't wanted to burden you. You're dealing with a difficult pregnancy and you already have a six-year-old girl and your husband is…" She patted my hand.

I hadn't told her much about the problems Jason and I were having. Right now, I needed her to focus, and I was more concerned with the corpse in the basement just then. "Mom, tell me what happened."

"He's been staying up late every night, glued to his computer. He knows that I wake up early in the morning, but he doesn't care." My mother searched my face for sympathy. "He's been disrupting my sleep, night after night."

"Okay, so tonight…?"

"Well, it was almost midnight and he hadn't come to bed. The television was blaring from the basement. I went downstairs and he was in front of that damned computer, clicking away. I turned off the television but he put it on again with the remote control. I turned it off and he did it again. He told me that if I didn't like it I could kiss his… well, his posterior. I went upstairs and got his gun. Then I came back and told him that if he didn't get up from that chair in ten seconds, I'd shoot him in the head. He wouldn't take me seriously. He said I was too stupid to pull the trigger. I told him I swore before God that I would shoot him if he didn't get away from the computer. He knew I would never make an oath and not follow through, but he didn't care. So I shot him."

I was on the verge of pointing out that she'd made an oath to love and honor Oscar, but she started crying and I put my arm around her. I guess she'd made an oath till death do they part, and Oscar had departed for good. I was both horrified and relieved. I'd wished Oscar dead a few times. The man had made a drunken pass at me at my own wedding. But I'd envisioned his car wrapped around a telephone pole, not a half-headed corpse minted by my mother's lucky shot. "We've got to figure out what to do."

"I'm telling the police it was self-defense," my mother sniffled.

"Mom, you shot Oscar in the back of the head. No one is going to believe you."

"Maybe he beat me."

"Did he, Mom?"

"Well… no. But he shouted at me." Her gray eyes regarded me hopefully. "He would even call me names, like the B-word."

"Bitch?"

"Claire! I raised you to be better than that."

My mother had just murdered her husband and she was lecturing me on deportment. "Mom, you're in serious trouble. The police aren't going to buy the idea that verbal abuse deserves a bullet."

"What should I do?"

"We'll make it look like a break-in. Come home with me and we'll pretend you were away when it happened. The neighborhood is getting bad, right? You've had three break-ins over the years." My mother started to protest but I talked her down. "Have you called anyone besides me? No? Where did the gun come from?"

"I don't know. Oscar got it two years ago. It wasn't registered."

"We'll take it with us and get rid of it before we get to St. Thomas."

My mother was nodding slowly. "But how did they get into the house?"

"We'll leave the doors unlocked."

"With the way things are going in this neighborhood, someone probably *will* break in."

My mother packed a bag for a weeklong visit, and we had a smooth drive to St. Thomas, stopping only once to toss the gun, wrapped in a tea towel, into Lake Ontario. We got to my place, a new house designed to look old, with a peaked-roof and wraparound porch, before sunrise. I led my mother to the guest room, gave her a sleeping pill, and tucked her in.

In my own bed I found Jason, asleep. Wondering what time he'd come home and whom he'd been with, I climbed in beside him, wishing I could take a sleeping pill. Of course I couldn't; it would have been bad for the baby. Instead I lay awake, feeling her kick for a while and planning what to tell my husband in the morning. I couldn't admit the truth about Oscar; Jason would have been first in line to rat out my mother, partly because he hated her, but also because he got along with Oscar. I'd have to think of a reason she appeared in the house overnight. It hit me then that Jason had come home late on Thursday, too. He was supposed to be out target shooting, but he hadn't crawled into bed till three. He'd gone running Friday morning and had barely grunted hello at me. I could pretend that my mother had arrived on Friday afternoon and he'd never know the difference. Since our daughter had gone straight to her sleepover party from school, she wouldn't say otherwise. I'd spoken to Maddie on Friday evening, but I could tell her that grandma and I were keeping her visit a secret surprise. Perfect, I thought as I drifted off.

The relief didn't last long. I was shaken awake by strong hands. "What the hell is going on?" Jason demanded. He was in his running gear, a tank top and shorts. Sunlight was just beginning to creep around the window shade.

"Stop shaking me! You could hurt the baby!"

Jason pulled back with a look of disgust. "Maybe that would be for the best. We could get rid of this one and try again for a boy."

We stared at each other in our familiar, hateful, face-off. Jason had been disappointed when Maddie was born because he'd wanted a boy. I'd had two miscarriages since then, and was so relieved when I made it past the rough point with this pregnancy. Then, a month ago, we'd found out we were having another girl. I was thrilled, but Jason's mood had been dark since then. This wasn't the first time he'd intimated that he hoped the baby wouldn't make it to term.

"What is *that woman* doing in my house?" He enunciated each word, as if I were as clueless as his freshman students.

"My mother is helping me with Maddie. It's not exactly easy taking care of a six-year-old when you're pregnant. Not that you'd know, since you've barely been home."

"Are we having that pity party again? Poor Claire, she just can't handle being pregnant."

I was having a tough pregnancy, complicated by serious hypertension. My ankles were permanently swollen, my hands so bloated that I couldn't wear my wedding ring. Maybe there was some poetic justice in that; Jason had stopped sporting his a long time ago.

"Keep your voice down," I said. "She's in the next room. She can hear you."

"I don't care what that old bitch hears! This is my house. Take her to a hotel."

"She's my mother and she'll be here for the next week.

Maddie will love it. She doesn't get to see enough of her grandmother."

"I am not having that woman watching me come and go."

"Guilty conscience?" I called after his retreating back. He slammed the bedroom door behind him.

Jason was in the kitchen, gulping down an energy drink, when I went downstairs. My mother sat at the table, nursing a cup of tea. "Good morning, dear," she chirped. "How did you sleep?"

"Not very well. What would you like for breakfast, Mom?"

"Don't you dare!" She got up. "I'm here to take care of you, Claire. Now sit down. Mama's restaurant is officially open."

"Thanks. I'll have scrambled eggs and toast, please."

"I'll have eggs, too," said Jason.

I glared at him, but my mother smiled politely. "Of course." She went to the fridge. "Would you like some orange juice?" she asked Jason as she poured a glass for me.

"I don't drink that crap. Power drinks rebalance your electrolytes properly."

"Oh, well, you're the gym teacher. I'm sure you know best."

"How many times have I told you not to call me a fucking gym teacher? I'm a kinesiologist at the University of Western Ontario. Got that?"

"I'm sorry, Jason. I didn't mean to offend you." My mother's voice was mild. "I just have trouble remembering… what was that word again?"

"Ki-ne-si-ol-o-gist."

"That's it."

Jason ate his eggs in silence, then went upstairs to shower.

"I'm sorry, Mom." I was embarrassed by his rudeness. "He's got a lot on his plate at work. It's a lot of stress, with everything going on."

"Oh, I'm sure, dear. These are difficult times." Her tone was reassuring but she wouldn't meet my eyes.

If Jason was obnoxious, Maddie was ecstatic. My mother came with me when I picked her up at her friend's house. "Grandma!" Maddie shrieked, then threw herself at my mother for a full-body hug.

"How's my precious angel?"

Back at home, after we'd stopped for ice cream, Maddie took my mother out to the backyard and let her ride her imaginary pony. I went upstairs, where Jason was on the phone. He hung up quickly when I walked into the bedroom. "What do you want?"

"I want to know if you're going to behave like a civilized person around my mother? You can't order her to make your breakfast."

"She's a guest in my house, she'll do what I say." He stood and went to his gym bag, unzipping it.

"What is your problem? I'm pregnant and you're supposed to be around. Instead you're out running around half the night with… with other people," I finished lamely.

"If you don't like it you can leave."

"This is my house, too."

"You're not paying the mortgage these days, so it's not yours."

"I'm taking some time off work, so that makes it your house?" True, I'd stopped working in my fifth month, when my doctor had ordered me on two weeks of bed rest. He was trying to lower my blood pressure, but everything Jason said and did jacked it up. I was on an unpaid leave at the moment. "You should at least be helping with Maddie! You're a useless excuse for a father."

Jason pulled one sneaker out of the gym bag and hurled it at me. I ducked to the right and it smacked against the wall with a heavy thud. He threw the other and it hit just as hard. We screamed at each other at the tops of our voices, hurling names and curses, before I finally stormed out of the room and back downstairs. Maddie was in the kitchen with my mother, drinking juice.

"Daddy throws things a lot," I heard her say. But when I came into the room, they gave me bright smiles and pretended nothing had happened.

*****

"If you were going to kill someone, how would you do it, Claire?" my mother asked me on Monday afternoon, while Maddie was at school and Jason was at work.

"That question is crazy." Since she'd come home with me, we'd avoided mentioning Oscar. With Maddie around, it was easy to pretend that Grandma was in for a regular visit. With her out of the house, it was hard to keep up the illusion.

"People never know what they're capable of until they're in a terrible situation. That's when your true character comes out." She was sitting at the table, polishing the silver tea service I'd inherited from my grandmother.

"What does that say about your character?"

"I think virtually anyone could be pushed to the point where they would kill someone." My mother's voice was philosophical, as if she were merely reflecting on an academic question that had little relevance to her own life. "And I think some people probably deserve to be killed."

"Mom! Whatever you do, don't ever say anything like that to Maddie."

"I wouldn't, dear, I promise." She polished the handle rigorously. "Claire, you don't know how much nonsense I put up with from that man for years. I was a ticking time bomb after living with him. But I wish I hadn't shot him."

"You're sorry he's dead?"

"No!" Mom exclaimed. "It was all so messy. The top of his head went *everywhere*. Ugh. It was like watching a pulpy melon explode." She shook her head. "If I had to do it all over again, I'd poison Oscar."

"What?"

"Really, it would be so much better. I've heard you can use antifreeze."

"Who told you that?"

"Beatrice McNully. That lady down the street from me with the wild English garden. Apparently antifreeze is very sweet. Animals lap it up off the side of the road and die. And you can mix it with sweet drinks."

"Beatrice McNully? The one whose husband died last year?" I was incredulous. "Did she kill him?"

"Well, I wouldn't blame her if she had. Thou shalt not

judge. You don't know how beastly men get as they get older, Claire. They're not fit to live in society."

"So you're going to bump them off?"

"Don't be silly." My mother's eyes had a faraway look. "We think it's fine to kill animals. Some people are alright with euthanizing sick people. Maybe there are others who need to be put out of their misery, too."

*****

On Thursday, we agreed that my mother would call the police out of concern for Oscar and his failure to return her calls. But she put it off, and on Friday morning we got a call out of the blue from the Toronto police. "Claire Wells? I'm sorry, but your stepfather is dead."

"What?" I gasped, genuinely shocked. How had they found out? Were they going to arrest my mother?

"It looks like a home invasion," the officer said. "There have been several in your parents' neighborhood. The house was robbed and vandalized. We haven't been able to locate your mother."

"She's staying with me right now. I'm pregnant and she's helping me with my six-year-old daughter."

I put my mother on the phone with the police and tried to call Jason from my cell. He didn't answer, which was typical. Since I didn't know whether he'd be willing or able to pick Maddie up from school, my mother and I had to pick her up and take her up to Toronto with us. "We're going on a road trip! Going on a ROAD TRIP!" she sang at the top of her lungs.

"Grandma has to tell you some sad news, sweetheart. Grandpa Oscar is dead."

"Really?" asked Maddie. "How?"

"Well, the police say some people broke into our house," my mother answered. I noticed her careful choice of words.

Maddie swung her legs against the seat. "Do you think I should I be sad?"

"You don't have to be anything, sweetie."

"Okay." She put her head on my mother's shoulder. "Are you sad, Grandma?"

"No, not really. But that's our secret."

*****

We met with the police in Toronto. Whoever had broken in had shot Oscar straightaway, they told us. His body was decomposing, already half-gone thanks to maggots, making it impossible to be precise about the day he died, let alone the time. The officers were solicitous towards my mother. When I saw pictures of what the home-invaders had done to the house, I understood why the police assumed that Oscar's corpse was also their handiwork. My mother's crystal and china were smashed, there were holes in the walls, and someone had spray-painted the walls with vaguely comprehensible profanity.

After we were done at the police station, and my mother had identified Oscar's remains, she hired the cleaning and home-repair service the police recommended and we checked into the Royal York. It was a treat for Maddie; she was never allowed to jump on beds at home. Our hotel suite had three, and she bopped from one room to the next. We went to a Disney animated movie and ate popcorn, then had pizza at an Italian restaurant.

That night, after Maddie was tucked into bed, my mother ordered tea for us from room service. "I feel positively decadent," she announced. "Oscar would have pushed me out the airshaft before he'd let me order room service."

"How are you holding up, Mom?"

"I keep thinking that I should feel terrible, but the truth is I don't." She put her head back and stared at the ceiling. "I feel bad about causing problems for you, and I'm angry that lowlifes wrecked my house. But when I think of Oscar, I'm just glad he's not going to be there when I go home."

"So what are you going to do with the next person who annoys you?"

"Don't be silly Claire. It's different when you live with someone. With a partner, I mean. When I married Oscar, it was because I was lonely. After your father died, it was just the two of us for years and years. Then you went away to school and it was just me, on my own. I was afraid, so I got married again. What a mistake."

"Did you feel that way from the start?"

"The day we married, I remember Oscar telling me he was happy because now he could really be himself. He presented such a different face to the world. He knew he was unlovable, the old warthog, so he pretended to be someone else. But the mask slips off. Sooner or later it does with everyone. But you know that, dear." She gave me a wan smile. "You've learned that yourself."

I didn't want to discuss Jason with her. "Mom, when Dad died, did you…"

"What, dear?"

It was hard to get the words out. "Did you have anything to do with it?"

"Oh, Claire!" One hand went to her chest as if I'd shot her through the heart. "How could you even think that?"

"I'm sorry, Mom. It's just… with everything going on… it just hit me."

She nodded and seemed to catch her breath. "It's alright, dear. I understand. It's just that I really did love your father."

*****

Oscar's funeral was a short ceremony at the St. James Cemetery Chapel. The priest quoted extensively from Scripture. "Oscar would have hated that," my mother gloated after the service. She'd been prim in a black suit and hat at the chapel, but when she got to her friend Beatrice McNully's house afterwards, she lost the hat, kicked off her shoes, and settled onto the sofa with a glass of champagne.

"Goodbye and good riddance," muttered Beatrice, clicking glasses with her. They giggled like naughty schoolgirls. My mother glanced at me and smiled. A blue-haired woman wearing more shiny gold jewelry than a strutting pimp would dare joined her on the couch. They clinked glasses and I thought I heard the bluish, blingy woman whisper *Congratulations.* But I couldn't be sure.

"Would you like a glass, dear?" asked Beatrice, handing me a crystal flute. "This one's just sparkling grape juice. Your mother told me you're having another girl. How delightful!" She was a wizened, wrinkled creature dressed all in purple, from her turban to her flowing caftan. Before I could answer, she turned to Maddie. "I hope you like chocolate milk, my dear. And lots of chocolate cake."

"Lots and lots of cake!" squealed Maddie. Beatrice took her by the hand and led her to the kitchen. I followed them, wondering if this woman really had murdered her husband. My mother had denied it when pressed, but her expression had said something else. Could the glass in my hand contain poison? Or what she was feeding my daughter…

Maddie was about to guzzle the chocolate milk when I knocked the glass out of her hand. She and Beatrice both stared at me in shock. "I'm so sorry," I mumbled. "Maddie's got a problem with lactose intolerance."

"Oh, I didn't realize. You poor little angel. Could I give her some pop instead?" asked Beatrice, her brow deeply furrowed. I knew it would make Maddie bounce off the walls, but since it was served out of a can, I figured it was safe, so I nodded, then knelt to mop up the spilled milk with a tea towel.

Beatrice waved me away. "A girl in your condition shouldn't even be on her feet," she proclaimed, then chased me back into the parlor. More women had arrived, and a row of champagne bottles had materialized on the mantelpiece. I looked at my mother, then at the women who were fussing over her and laughing with her. They all seemed to be somewhere between fifty-five and seventy-five, and while their styles were individual, there was a definite preference for bright colors and mounds of jewelry.

I heard a low chuckle beside me. "Shot his fool head off! Who would've thought it?" She gave me a broad smile straight out of a denture cream ad and patted my arm, then went over to hug my mother.

"So, is Freddie still in a coma?" I heard one woman ask another. I turned my head, and for a moment, I felt as if I were surrounded by a group of black widow spiders. Gleeful spiders, sprung from the bonds of matrimony by unholy acts. But that was ridiculous. These women couldn't have killed their husbands. Okay, my mother had done just that… and maybe Beatrice… but the rest…

Pleading a headache, I grabbed Maddie and ran. My mother didn't come back to the hotel until late that evening. When she did, she was too tipsy to really talk, though she did slur, "Everyone agrees I have the *best* daughter!"

*****

"We need to go back home and see Daddy," I told Maddie the next morning.

"Why?" she retorted. "He's always yelling. Then he throws things." She threw her arms around my legs. "Let's stay at grandma's. It's fun with the three of us."

My mother — whom I'd expected to be hung over, yet who seemed oddly fresh and vibrant — suggested that I go home while Maddie stayed with her. "See if you can work things out. If you can, then wonderful. If you can't… Well, there's counseling, I suppose."

"Maddie has to go to school, Mom. We're going home."

We got back to St. Thomas that afternoon. I felt such a surge of relief when I saw our house. It was good to leave my mother and her set of crazies behind and embrace the familiar. Maddie had sulked most of the drive home, but she ran through the house with an exuberant "Wheeeeee!" that made me laugh. Even she was glad to be home.

The house itself was a mess. Dirty dishes lined the counter, and clothing that reeked of sweat lay in the bathroom. I loaded the dishwasher and started a load of laundry. There was a red thong that I knew wasn't mine mixed in with Jason's workout gear. It wasn't really a surprise. He'd long been spending half the night out of the house, so bringing one of his floozies back here didn't seem out of character. But now I was back, and he wouldn't be doing that again.

While I was cleaning the bathroom, Maddie came in, eyes wide. "Mommy, don't be mad at me."

"Why would I be mad at you, honey?"

"I broke something."

"Are you hurt?" I took her hands in mine, but she shook her head.

"No, in Daddy's office. He's going to be so mad!"

"Let's go see."

Jason had forbidden Maddie to ever go into his office, but it had a computer and she and I had an unspoken agreement that it was okay to go in there when Daddy wasn't home. There was an open cardboard box lying under the desk, and dozens of small vials spilled all over the rug.

I knelt to pick them up, wondering when Jason had started using steroids. "Tell me what happened, Maddie."

"I was just swinging my legs." She pointed at the chair. "I was there, and it was on the shelf under the desk. Then those things went rolling everywhere. Are you mad?"

"No, I'm not mad at you," I said.

"I can help pick them up," she announced, smiling.

"No, honey. You go to your room right now and play there. Mommy will take care of this."

After she left I examined a vial. *Oxytocin IP,* it read. My mind reeled. Wasn't that the drug known as hillbilly heroin? Was that what Jason was taking? No, that was OxyContin. The box was plain except for a white label with a return address in Vancouver. I was tempted to throw the whole thing in the garbage, but afraid of Jason's reaction. After I put the box back under the desk, I typed the name of the drug into a search engine.

"Oxytocin, generic Pitocin, makes the muscles of the uterus contract, helping to push out your baby…"

The words didn't make much sense at first. Not until I looked at the computer's web cache. Jason had been spending a lot of time on sites that explained how to induce a late-term miscarriage. Oxytocin was colorless and flavorless, one site noted. Easy to mix with another liquid. Results guaranteed.

I'd already had two miscarriages. Both girls, both gone. *These things happen,* a doctor had told me. *Sometimes we never find out why.*

But sometimes we do.

I don't know how long I sat there, absorbing the details. But when I got up, I went straight to the kitchen and pulled on a pair of rubber gloves. It wasn't hard to find what I needed. My mother had purchased gallons of antifreeze, which she'd left on the back porch. I'd always thought antifreeze was blue, but my mother had found it in a rainbow of colors, including green and orange. I admired her ability to plan ahead. Back in the kitchen, I found four containers of the energy drink Jason swore by in the fridge, two already open. I took a little from one into a glass, then poured half of the liquid down the drain. Then I opened the antifreeze and filled the container. Half-and-half, I thought, that seems about right. I repeated the process with each container, carefully color-coordinating. Maybe Jason would notice that a couple of the new bottles were open, I worried, then remembered that when Jason was thirsty, nothing got between him and his power drinks.

I finished up and put the antifreeze back in the garage. Then I went to Maddie's room. "Guess what, sweetheart? We have to go back to Grandma's."

"Really?" Maddie jumped in obvious delight.

"We'll get dinner on the drive back," I promised. "We can't eat anything in the house. Daddy let all the food go bad."

Then I went to the basement and called my mother. "Are you absolutely, completely positive that antifreeze really kills people?"

"Yes, dear." Her voice was calm, and not at all surprised, as if I'd called to ask her for an update on the weather forecast. Maybe it wasn't a surprise, though. She'd been the one who'd bought all that antifreeze. "I'm positive. Beatrice McNully says it takes a few hours, even a day, and that the victim will act drunk."

I almost dropped the phone. Beatrice really had killed her husband. But all I said was, "Drunk?"

"Well, they're dying of alcohol poisoning, after all. They get disoriented, then drop dead quite suddenly. It's *very* hard to trace." There was a question lurking in her voice, but she didn't ask it. She knew what I'd done. She'd helped me do it, really.

She was my accomplice, just as I'd been hers.

"Okay," I mumbled. "Thanks, Mom."

"You're welcome, Claire." Her voice was warm and gentle. She didn't say *Welcome to the club,* but I knew that was what she was thinking.

A Sting in the Tail
Pauline Gostling

From the upstairs hotel window, I watched the waves, suspended between dark and light, crash over the distant shoreline. Ever since Michael had admitted to the affair, things had been difficult. So here I was, trying to rekindle the flame of our less that perfect marriage. It was our third anniversary, and he had to attend the Health and Safety Symposium in Brighton. So I had phoned ahead, arranging for a key to be left so I could surprise him. This was his last chance and I *so* wanted it to work.

In the bathroom, I carefully unpacked new lingerie from my overnight bag. Undressing quickly, untying my hair so it fell to my shoulders, studying my reflection in the full-length mirror, I was not impressed. That was about to change. Sucking in my stomach, I stepped into the suspender belt, twisting it around my waist, then the panties. Ah, the panties. A trade description misnomer if ever there was one, but I got into them! Should I have gone for the scarlet? No, too tacky, although the black did look a bit harsh against my fair skin and brown hair. Then the tights. The bra achieved the lift and forward thrust I had hoped for, even if my breasts did spill over the top. Still, the cleavage was impressive! Looking sideways at myself I refused to feel deflated, grinning in the mirror at my unfortunate choice of word. The shoes I *loved,* even if they did kill me. Hopefully I wouldn't be wearing them for long. Just, a measured sashay to the bed before kicking them off. I had taken advice from the beautician in John Lewis and thrown out my ancient cosmetics. Well, not quite all! The new items were expensive, but hopefully, worth it. New perfume too - subtle, sophisticated, just what I was aiming for. Carefully removing the ornate stopper I sprayed it on my wrist. It hadn't seemed that strong in the shop. Then, I heard footsteps. And voices.

Holding my breath I quickly pulled the bathroom door closed, switching off the light, listening hard.

I could make out two voices, one definitely Michael's, the other a woman's. The apartment door clicked open, a finger of light sweeping under the bathroom door. I put my ear against it, there wasn't a keyhole.

They were laughing, "Thought the silly old sod wouldn't ever shut up!" Michael's soft Irish brogue more pronounced, animated.

"I know! Always the same. Likes the sound of his own voice."

Didn't sound like her natural voice, hard to tell as she was slurring her words. I visualised some blonde, well veneered trollop, huge breasts hanging out, knock-out perfume and high heels (probably like the ones I was struggling with at the moment - but he was *my husband!*). I released my breath slowly.

There was silence, then his voice. "I'll get my phone charger for you." Footsteps. "Here you go. There's no rush, I've got a spare."

"Thanks Michael." Drawing out his name, she was just *too* grateful. Conniving cow.

"Ah that's ok." I visualised his smug, deprecating smile. "Where's your room?" Are you on this floor?" My heart sank. Was he really that stupid?

"Don't know." Listening to her coy giggle, imagining over made-up tart's eyes staring, unfocused, into his … my stomach turned.

"What's your room number?"

"Can't remember. Have to check." Further flirtatious giggle. "Whoops! Oh dear now I've dropped it." Something small clattered to the floor, then his footsteps crossing the tiles. "Steady Claire, let me help you." He must have picked up the passkey. "Room 1347. I think you're on this floor. Come on, up you get." I imagined *my* husband hauling Ms Slapper to her feet, transfixed on her voluptuous cleavage.

"Let's find your room shall we?"

Oh, yes *let's* Michael - you bloody fool! I could feel the veins in my head pulsating, the tension making me feel strung out like the strings on a violin, waiting for the downward sweep of the bow. I stuffed my fist to my mouth, to stop myself screaming, to stop myself charging out of the bathroom and confronting them.

"You do smell nice, Michael! You can come closer you know." Her voice dropping seductively. Was it the *Ambre Nuit*, I had bought him? I seethed. That was so expensive!

"Ah, this is what I miss. The closeness. It's so hard …," she purred.

I caught sight of myself in the low lit mirror, my chest rising and falling like a bellows.

"You know we're not together anymore don't you? I've left him." Was *she* the one he'd had the affair with? Without waiting for his reply she continued, "Don't like being on my own, Michael. Can't sleep." I imagined her draped against him, fawning all over him. Her slurred attempt to be coquettish made me want to vomit, and there I was, fingers now welded to the bathroom door handle. What should I do? Fly out of the bathroom in full trollop attire, a mad woman wanting revenge? However, the decision was soon made for me.

"Come on, let's find your room." *Would* he just see her to her room?

"We could have another drink first?" She protested, but he must have pulled her to the door as I could hear stumbling against the furniture. Then footsteps and her querulous voice, fading down the corridor.

Unpeeling my fingers from the handle, I switched on the light, my reflection coming back at me, white with shock. Cheap, tacky and overdone. Grabbing a long stream of toilet paper, the rest of the roll unravelling on the floor, I rubbed at the make-up, smearing it around my face. Colours smudged, streaking my cheeks. I looked grotesque. Why hadn't I thought to bring make up remover? I scrubbed at my skin but the waterproof mascara was just that, leaving dark rings around my eyes. I didn't care anymore. Angrily I flushed the paper down the toilet. The sound of seams ripping as I struggled out of the outfit gave me inordinate satisfaction. What now? Was he coming back? Or was it happening again?

Time passed. Five, ten – twenty minutes and still I waited. And waited – watching from the window where, earlier, I had stood with such hope. Now, gazing to the shoreline, all I could see was blackness. Like my heart.

I had my answer. He wasn't coming back.

*****

It was shortly after lunch on the Sunday when he came home. I was at the sink drying dishes. He looked tired as he offered me the flowers. Drying my hands on the tea towel, I took them, sinking my nose into the soft rose petals. They had no perfume, I laid them on the worktop.

"Thanks. So, how did it go?" I was very formal.

"Usual. Boring."

Sensing my mood, he tried to make more of an effort. "Sorry I missed your call yesterday. I was going to ring you back but it was late. Thought you might be asleep." Lifting his gaze from the roses sheathed in cellophane, he turned to me. "Did you get my text, saying I was leaving?"

"Yes."

Sighing, running his hand through his hair, "I'm sorry Amy."

I turned to face him, propping my back against the draining board, masking my hurt and anger. "I was worried. You left your EpiPen here."

"Yeah, realised too late. There's a pharmacy in Brighton which was able to fill my emergency prescription. Sent it round to the hotel by same day courier." Self-consciously he ran a finger around his collar, easing it from his throat. "Stupid of me but I was OK." Grabbing his bag he made for the door. "I'll just take this upstairs."

"You were lucky," I said, stretching to put some plates in the cupboard.

*****

Over the next few weeks, suspended between truth and reality – frozen in time like an insect embedded in amber – my resentment grew. I was barely able to look him in the eye. Several times I mentioned his trip to Brighton, hoping to catch him out. But he wasn't forthcoming, only bored that I kept referring back to it. He did know *something* was wrong though, and tried to please me. And, yes, I played on it.

*****

On a glorious June morning a few weeks later, shading my eyes, I glanced through the window. "Garden looks a mess and the shears need sharpening. Last time I tried using them they were too blunt to cut anything."

"I'll do it." Glad of any opportunity to help, he followed me to the shed. The smell of earth, damp wood, and a whiff of decay escaping, meeting me as I unlocked the door.

Looking between discarded pots and overturning tools, he asked, "d'you know where they are?"

Brushing aside a cobweb, I lifted the shears from a bucket.

"Here. I'll make us a cup of tea before I start on the lawn". As I stepped out into the sunshine, I tried slamming the door closed. Only the door catch didn't catch and the door swung open again, pushing me forward, as it always did! Tutting I walked back to the house.

*****

I had to nudge aside pots and tools to make room for the tray on the workbench when I returned. Michael was concentrating, running the blade of the shears back and forth over the old grinder, which zinged and hummed under pressure from his fingers. I drank my tea, watching coloured sparks and dust motes spin in the air. Seeing me place my cup back on the tray he reached for his.

"No rush." I said, over my shoulder, picking up the tray. Stepping outside, pushing the door closed with a nudge from my hip – only to have the wretched thing swing open again as usual, lurching me forward, jarring my back.

Pauline Gostling

I was annoyed. "We still haven't fixed this damn door have we? I'll have to close it while I mow round the shed." Before he could answer I slammed it shut, ramming the hasp over the staple and sliding the padlock into place. "Bloody thing. That should hold it." I stood back, staring hard at the lock, wiping my hands on my trousers before heading for the mower.

Maintaining straight lines and navigating the borders took time. It must have taken me over an hour to finish the lawn, and I was hot and sweaty. I'd quite forgotten Michael locked in the shed. The cranky old mower, that we'd been meaning to replace for years, was so noisy I wouldn't have heard him if he had called.

Stretching my aching back, scraping cut grass from my shoes I went back to the shed. Removing the padlock, the door swung open, dry hinges squeaking in protest, like fingernails down a blackboard. I was expecting noise, movement, Michael bemoaning the fact he had been locked in. But there was only silence. He lay on the floor, tools scattered around him, his face swollen, tongue protruding through puffy lips.

When I saw the battered hornets crawling nearby on the shed floor I knew he was dead. Highly sensitive, he would have reacted to the stings in seconds. Franticly I stamped on them, putting my anger to good use against the horrible insects, then I shut and locked the door again before heading into the house to phone the Emergency Services.

Later I was told by friends that I kept repeating, "He must have forgotten his EpiPen again!" over and over and over.

*****

The funeral had been and gone, and I was trying to get on with my life. That changed the day *she* came to the house. The moment she opened her mouth, that same fake accent, even though this time she probably wasn't sozzled, I knew it was her. She looked nothing like the trollop I'd imagined, having to admit she looked quite presentable for an *older* woman. She muttered something about being abroad at the time of the funeral so couldn't attend. As if I cared! I couldn't believe the cheek of the woman!

Rather than show myself up on my own doorstep I allowed her in. We perched opposite each other, in silence. I waited.

She spoke first. "He was a lovely man." She gushed. "You must miss him so much. He was always kind to me at work you know …"

"So I believe." Carefully I enunciated each word. "You must have been very grateful when he took you back to your room after the Brighton conference."

Eyes wide, her head shot back.

"After you dropped your room pass?" I added for maximum impact.

She looked confused. "Oh, he told you then?"

Looking her straight in her eyes, "…and how you and he spent the night together …"

Struggling to stand, raising her hands to protect herself. "Oh no. You've got it all wrong," shaking her head in disbelief, "it wasn't *anything* like that. He just … helped me to my room."

"Really!" I stood up. I wasn't tall enough to stand over her so crossed my arms. "You must think I'm stupid. I don't know how you've got the nerve to come here." Taking pleasure at the fear in her eyes, feeling like a gladiator before he delivers the killer blow. "I know the two of you spent the night together, so it's no good denying it."

Looking at me strangely, collapsing back into the armchair,

she spoke softly. "You don't know do you?"

"Know what?" Head thrust forward, I waited.

"You think … him, and me?" shaking her head, taking a deep breath, she continued quietly. "No, you're wrong. Michael and Robbie …, were together. Had been for … ooh, I don't know for how long … It was common knowledge at work, so I assumed you knew! I'm so sorry."

Moving away to drown out her hated voice, I remembered. The shed, the large hornets, and how wrong I'd been to assume the end would ever have justified the means.

Bridget Reilly's Hero
Linda Kerr

Scandi Noir is so last year, thought Bridget as she reached for the (far too conveniently placed) biscuit tin. Perhaps she should hide those biscuits, maybe in the next ad break. She couldn't move now, not while her favourite detective, Eliza Tereschova from Belarus was in danger. Eliza, with her brilliant mind, athletic body and erratic social skills, always seemed to succeed where her more traditional colleagues failed. In this episode, clad in her signature motorbike leathers, Eliza had been enticed into the woods by a seemingly charming, slightly alarming, very blond man. *What's the betting*, Bridget wondered, *if this murder isn't linked to the terrible atrocities committed in those woods during the war? And the blond lad could well turn out to be a Nazi sympathiser.*

You'd think Eliza would have learnt by now but no, she was a sucker for those cheekbones and that's how she found herself right at the site of the wartime massacre with nothing but her police issue revolver and her own razor-sharp reactions.

The forest was, in turn, pitch black or bleached by flashlights. The tall conifers and their spiky boughs, though providing incredibly beautiful snowflake effects, made it difficult for Bridget to concentrate on the tense story line. For such a grisly monument those woods were exceptionally scenic and she made a mental note to add Belarus to her lengthening list of potential destinations should she ever feel free to travel again.

There were many strange noises in the forest; swishing of branches, twigs snapping under foot, a tap-tapping at a window–

There were no windows in the forest. Bridget turned down the volume on the TV.

Tap-tap. Tap-tap. It was coming from the lounge window. From the other side of the secure lock behind the blackout blinds and curtains. There it was again, Tap-tap, tap-tap. It didn't exactly sound like a human trying to get in. She hoped it wasn't. She hoped there was a plausible reason for this strange sound. But she couldn't think of any. It certainly wasn't a neighbour coming to call. The police had been very clear with their advice; *'For the time being making friends is not your priority. Staying safe is more important'*, and Bridget had carefully followed all the advice she'd been given. She wasn't going to risk her hard-won safety.

Tap-tap.

It sounded for all the world like a bird trying to find its way, a big bird, perhaps a magpie, feeling with its beak or claws for an escape route, or a way into the house. Bridget's stomach automatically clenched and simmered, momentarily bringing to mind the crater of Vesuvius, where they'd taken the boys, years ago, on one of those expensive, educational, meticulously planned holidays. Oh, why didn't she leave him earlier? She'd thought she was protecting those poor kids by staying. She knew better now.

Tap-tap, tap-tap. Lower down the window now.

She hoped against hope that it was only a bird and, practicing her breathing exercises, she edged across the room where the TV screen showed the tall blond man (she'd been right about him all along) stalking Eliza through the trees; a stark, pale light-form against the dark, earthy foliage.

Bridget crept to the window. Her hand itched to lift the curtain, to take one peek outside, but she couldn't risk it. Anyone outside would see her clearly while she would be unable to see them. She held her breath – all the better to hear – and detected a faint change in tone of the taps.

Were they moving?

Yes, she thought, they tracked very slowly from glass to window frame, and then across the wall to the door frame. Whoever it was, they were now outside the front door.

Whoever it was? Bridget almost laughed. She knew perfectly well who it was but she had to be sure. Making her way into the kitchen, which was in complete darkness, she could peer through to the hall.

How she wished she hadn't. Silhouetted there against the glass, tap, tap, tapping on the door, was a shape she knew as well as her own reflection. She'd spent 25 years sleeping with him, waking with him, eating with him, screaming at him, pleading, watching, waiting and finally, escaping to this little house of her own hundreds of miles away.

She couldn't let Frank see her. As soon as he did, she was done for. He would know just by looking at her how to get back, what buttons to press, what knives to sharpen, what bones to break. She heard a dull sound, a container, maybe, being dragged over the ground and dumped onto the front step. There was the scrape of the letter box hinge being raised.

'For feck's sake...' he lisped, frustration building up, as always. She waited for him to punch the door and, sure enough, he did. When she'd screwed that metal plate in place behind the letter box she was sure that she was being ridiculous. She'd followed the police instructions but, all the time, she told herself: *Frank might be violent. He might want to hurt you. He might be able to track you down all these miles away but surely he'd never... he'd never set fire to the place. Would he?*

The Bridget who used to be married to Frank wanted to curl into a ball, like the tiny hedgehog she'd found in her new garden. She wanted to sink into the foundations of this new, 'safe' house and, at first, she did, flattening herself on the kitchen floor, trying to make herself as small as possible. It was as if the tap-tapping was snaking through the front door, along the brickwork, burrowing into the plasterwork and along the tiles, tap-tapping its way into her body, into her heart. But while she lay there shaking, she felt something new. Where before Frank had turned her insides to mush – first in a good way, then horrifyingly so – now she could feel her heart pounding. Only this time it was solid and strong, as dense as a walnut kernel, beating regularly, all on its own, protecting itself and keeping her body alive. The kernel grew as she breathed, deeply, slowly, drowning out the tapping noise which continued, unheard. Something different was happening. Was this what they called courage? She knew now, in her body as well as her mind, that those things they had told her; that she deserved a life of her own, that she could live without fear, that she could do something, anything, whatever it took, to stop him getting in. Those things were true.

Mentally, she reviewed her home; the double locks on the door, the window reinforcements and the panic button just six feet away from her left hand. All she had to do was scoot across the room and press the button.

On screen, Eliza was back in her office, galvanising the troops for one last attempt to arrest the murderer, strapping on a Kevlar vest and loading her revolver. Bridget took a deep breath, girded her loins and pressed the button. She couldn't hear the tapping any more but that could mean anything. He could be standing there still, waiting until she, feeling safer, opened the door to look out. He could stare her out in any competition. She had always blinked first, in the past.

In the past there had been nowhere to run. In the past she'd had no option but to, eventually, open the door. But now, Bridget realised, she could stand her ground. *This house is safe*, she told herself. *As safe as it ever could be*. Perhaps she should ring the emergency number just to make sure the alarm had got through to the right people? Just to hear someone's voice. She stood up, breathing in and squaring her shoulders as she'd learnt. Picking up her phone from the coffee table, she lifted it smartly to her ear. The emergency operator replied within two rings, saying:

'I'm going to stay right here on the line until the officers get there.'

*****

Bridget heard Frank pleading innocence as he tried to reason with the police 'You know how it is…', and he begged them to let him have, 'just one word with my wife, please' but, on this occasion, it didn't work. The police found the petrol can, the plastic tube and the matches. He wasn't going to wriggle out of this one so easily. People believed her now.

On the screen Eliza Tereschova took aim and the killer died in a hail of bullets.

Police Officer Turner, busy reviewing security and making sure Bridget was safe, at least for the time being, paused and followed Bridget's gaze.

'Oh, I love this show,' she said, 'Don't we all want to be Eliza, deep down?'

Bridget smiled. She wasn't quite so powerful yet, but she was getting there.

Death in the Kingdom of Pines

Kate Miller

Chapter 1

Les Houches, Haute Savoie, France, February 1931

Marie-Laure stared at the brandy placed in front of her. She had never drunk brandy in daylight before. All she could see was, not his face, but a pine cone, splattered with blood, lying in the snow. *The bastard*, she said to herself. *The out and out bastard.*

And the day had started so well.

*****

I'm going to work, Marie-Laure Monaghan told herself as she came out of the forest and stopped to put on her skis. An icy wind off the glaciers on Mont Blanc hit the back of her neck and she shivered. But as she looked across the valley of white snow and black pines to the towering rocks beyond, excitement rose up in her. *I'm going to work.*

It was not yet eight o'clock and the sun was still behind the mountains. Below her was a stretch of snow, at the bottom a row of buildings, including a café where glass doors gave access to a small terrace with views up the slope. Beyond the buildings was the road to Chamonix. Until three years ago, this modest hillside had been the field where the pigs were kept. Now it was a ski piste. A nursery slope admittedly, and one crisscrossed with tracks and pitted with holes where beginners had been overcome by gravity, but recognisably a piste. It had its part in the unstoppable craze for skiing which was sweeping the French Alps, bringing money and glamour to downtrodden villages, dragging the bemused inhabitants out of their dark chalets and turning the deathly Alpine winter into a season of speed and fun.

And for Marie-Laure, this slope was now her workplace. She buckled on her skis, then hesitated, suddenly aware that anyone in the café would be able to look out and watch her descending. New pupils could be seeing her, their ski instructor, arriving for work. Suppose she fell? Her face burned with imagined humiliation. It was too early for pupils to have arrived but her fellow instructors might already be there. The thought of them gave her a fierce determination to ski the short slope beautifully. So she did.

At the bottom, she took off her skis and leaned them on the newly-built rack. She knocked on the glass doors and young Pierrot let her in. She went to warm her hands by the iron stove that filled the café with welcome heat.

The place was quiet. 'Where's Harald?' she asked.

Pierrot shrugged. 'Out for an early run I suppose,' he said. 'No lessons until half past nine.'

'Actually I'm giving an early morning lesson.'

Pierrot shrugged again, with what she was sure was a deliberate lack of interest.

She continued, determined not to let him spoil her important day, 'I'm expecting my client in about fifteen minutes, so can I have a cup of coffee first?'

Pierrot gaped at her. She wasn't sure if he was being rude or just stupid. Probably both. He was a gangly youth who opened up the café for Harald in the mornings, manned the bar at night and helped out with ski lessons during the day. He wasn't exactly an instructor, in her view.

'You want some coffee?' he said. 'I thought all you English girls drank tea.'

'I'm not English,' she said firmly. 'We've been through this already.'

Pierrot poured a café au lait and placed it in front of her on the bar. She sipped the coffee, looking out at the snow as she waited for God's Gift. The clock ticked to 8.15. 8.20. He was late.

'Your pupil's late,' Pierrot said, unafraid to state the obvious. 'Who is it anyway?'

'It's Monsieur Siebert. Um, quite a loud man...' Marie-Laure searched for words to describe him without sounding ungracious. So what if he was a balding show-off who fancied himself as God's Gift to Women, and had pinched her bottom when he booked the lesson? A paying pupil was a good pupil.

'The pushy poseur with the big moustache?' Pierrot grinned. 'He's probably still in bed with a hangover. If it's the bloke I'm thinking of, he was in here till past midnight last night, completely legless.'

Marie-Laure's heart sank. That sounded like her man.

The *Café des Sports* was an old-fashioned place, with a tiled floor and hard metal chairs. It took up one corner of a plain, square building which fronted onto the main road. Once, it had been the *Bar des Houches*, where men in blue overalls sat over their red wine, smoked their cigarettes, and where women never ventured. But three years before, it had been bought by the famous ski champion Harald Sigurssen, renamed the *Café des Sports* and turned into the hub of his ski school.

There was a rush of cold air as the door opened and Harald

entered, full of vigour from his early morning run. But he glowered as he looked around the café.

'Where is everybody?'

'Jean-Luc is giving an early lesson,' Pierrot said.

'And Raymond?'

'Er, Raymond is…'

At that moment the front door opened and a bulky figure came in.

'Late!' barked Harald.

Raymond took off his coat and offered no apology, just settling himself on a stool at the bar. Pierrot sniggered, like a naughty schoolboy protected by his bigger friend. Harald was prevented from saying more as the front door opened again and five men entered, carrying skis and dressed in tweeds and thick jerseys. Harald raised a hand to get their attention. 'If you gentlemen would follow me,' and took them over to his office – a designated table in the far corner of the bar. Marie-Laure knew it wouldn't be long before he was giving them his usual introductory talk on the benefits of the Harald Sigurssen ski tuition method.

'Not working this morning Marie-Laure?' asked Raymond.

'She's waiting for her pupil,' said Pierrot.

'Oh yes, your rich guy. He hasn't turned up? What a shame. Maybe he's not happy with the, er, service you're providing. Maybe you should have given him what he wanted.'

Marie-Laure sat stony faced.

Egged on by Raymond, Pierrot said, 'Maybe she did give him what he wanted, and now he doesn't need to bother with a ski lesson just to get a poke.'

'What was he like then Marie-Laure?' Raymond persisted. 'Big is he? Hung like a horse, I bet.'

'I wouldn't know,' she said, trying to sound as neutral as possible.

'Come on,' said Raymond. 'You're not at the convent now. You won't get pupils by acting like a nun.'

She wasn't going to rise to this. 'He's just late,' she said.

'Oh well, of course, he was planning to do a warm-up run before he had his lesson with you,' Raymond said casually. 'Didn't he tell you? He mentioned it when we were chatting at the bar last night. I told him to drop into the P'tit Alpe while he was up there. You know Old Pascal is selling his pear brandy from behind the cowshed now. Just the thing to get you going in the morning.'

Suddenly Harald was there behind them. 'Enough! You two,' he pointed at Raymond and Pierrot. 'I've got clients here expecting to start their morning's lesson. Now get going. My ski school has a reputation to maintain.'

'We haven't finished our coffee…' Pierrot whined.

'Fuck off out of here!'

They left and once again the bar was quiet. 'Idiots,' sighed Harald. 'And why are you still here Marie-Laure?'

'I'm still waiting for Monsieur Siebert to appear. Apparently he was very drunk last night.'

'But I saw him,' Harald said. 'An hour ago – more. He was heading this way, carrying his skis. Said he'd booked an early lesson and was going up the mountain road for a practice run first.'

Marie-Laure looked out at the slopes. 'I'll go and find him. He might have got lost.' She got up and reached for her jersey.

'Surely he can look after himself,' said Harald. 'He told me he'd been a telemark champion in the Jura and was just coming to us for a little refresher course.'

'He told me that too. But in truth he can barely stand up on his skis.' She pulled her jersey over her head and started for the door. 'I'd better go and track him down.'

'Yes, that'd be for the best,' Harald said grimly. 'If he breaks a leg he might not pay.'

*****

Outside she picked her skis off the rack. At nearly two metres, they were much taller than her. Catching sight of her reflection in the café window, she considered the effect, with dissatisfaction.

The top half wasn't too bad: her dark bobbed hair, together with the sunglasses, was worthy of Coco Chanel. Even down to her neat waist she looked rather *gamine*, she thought. But there was no disguising her unfashionably round hips and lamentably un-coltish legs. God's Gift to Women had made a pass at her after the first lesson. But then he probably made a pass at anyone under the age of 50 who didn't actually have to shave in the morning.

She looked up. A figure had appeared out of the trees at the top of the nursery slope. Normally this slope was her domain, where she was either persuading nervous newcomers to point their skis downhill and slide a little way – just a little way – or else discouraging over-confident speed-seekers from zooming straight down and right through the French windows of the *Café des Sports*.

Was it Monsieur Siebert, at last? But no, this was an expert skier, zigzagging casually, followed by two knock-kneed shapes descending very slowly. Her stomach did a somersault. It was Jean-Luc. But she was going to stay calm.

Instead of setting off, she waited until Jean-Luc glided to a halt in front of her. 'Not working this morning Marie-Laure?'

he said. His sarcastic grin attracted and repelled her, as ever.

'Shouldn't you be helping them?' she asked, indicating his two charges, one of whom was now flailing around on the ground while the other tried to help him up with a ski pole.

Jean-Luc threw them a glance. 'They learn more when they make their own mistakes,' he said. 'Couldn't Harald find you a pupil this morning? You can't be a ski instructor without pupils Marie-Laure.'

'Actually I have a pupil. Monsieur Siebert.'

'The one that Pierrot calls the pushy poseur with the big moustache?'

'That's him. He booked an early lesson but hasn't turned up. Apparently he went out for a warm-up run.'

'Yes – we saw him,' Jean-Luc said.

She sighed. Everybody had seen him except her, his instructor. 'Where exactly did you see him?'

'At the top of the road.'

'Was he alright?' she asked.

'His technique was rubbish but I didn't stop to criticise. I assumed he was going to do what we did and ski back down the track. We had quite a few, er, rests, so I expected him to overtake us, but he didn't.'

Marie-Laure sighed again. 'I think he's getting stuck into the pear brandies.' She put on her gloves.

Jean-Luc winked at her. 'Let me dump these two and I'll come with you.' Behind him she could see his two clients had collapsed in a heap, their glasses steamed up and a faint mumbling coming from their mouths.

'No thanks,' Marie-Laure said crisply. 'You really ought to go over a few basics with them.'

She didn't want Jean-Luc around; she didn't need him. What there had been between them was over and that was how she wanted it to stay. And really there had been nothing between them. She didn't care about Jean-Luc one way or the other. She repeated this to herself a few times.

Shouldering her skis, she set off along the track, which in summer was a dirt road leading up to Old Pascal's farm, the P'tit Alpe. She liked walking. Her leather boots, though heavy, gripped the snow well and her Norwegian ash skis – they had to be ash, Harald insisted – were light to carry.

Amongst the trees, she inhaled the scent of pine, the perfumed breath of the mountain, and felt the rush it always gave her. Her feet crunched in fresh snow. Shafts of sunlight filtered through the trees, dappling the ground with shadows. It was a glorious day.

She still felt surprised that this was a Wednesday, in February, and she was out in the forest instead of in the classroom at Sainte Thérèse, teaching English grammar to Junior Four. A background feeling that she should be at work nagged her. But she was at work – she was a ski instructor now. The convent school was behind her. She had a wonderful new job.

But would it stay wonderful if she made a mess of this? If she discovered God's Gift sitting over a bottle of *poire* at the P'tit Alpe and he told her to get lost. What the hell made her think he was going to pay a woman to teach him when he could ski perfectly well, as everyone could see…

Well, Harald would back her up. Nobody argued with Harald. Tall, lean, his dark hair grey now, his fierce brows and hooked nose giving him the air of a brooding eagle, he barked orders in his Norwegian-accented French and his pupils obeyed without question. Nobody argued with Harald's three international gold medals in ski jumping and two in long distance ski racing.

As she walked up the road, she could see tracks, but only of one skier. Jean-Luc and his pair of pupils had turned off onto the slope, rather than follow the road all the way down to the village. Had Monsieur Siebert simply given up and gone back to his hotel, without bothering to call into the café? Was he so disappointed with his lesson, or with her?

The road wound uphill and she began to feel warm, even though by now she was completely in the shade of the trees and could barely see the sun. The ground was treacherous: every now and then she slipped on a patch of ice. Tracks showed that various skiers had come down, this morning or the day before.

Damn Monsieur Siebert! She should never have gone near the arrogant boor. But he was ready to pay good money and he was her first real client, as she saw it. Rather than just being a pupil handed to her by Harald or one of the other instructors, Monsieur Siebert had driven up to the ski school in his sports car, asking for her – the lady ski instructor. Jean-Luc and the others had sniggered but she knew they were envious. Up till then they had tolerated her as useful for taking the kind of pupils they didn't want to teach. 'Nervous types,' Jean-Luc had said. 'Little kids, spinsters.' The sort who wouldn't tip. The sort who were not seeking Harald's rugged glamour or Jean-Luc's practised charm or Raymond and Pierrot's…. What exactly *did* Raymond and Pierrot have to offer, she wondered? They were local lads, 'strong boys who know these mountains,' Harald said approvingly. When she had landed God's Gift, with his swagger and ready cash, they had been seething.

It had not taken her long to realise that Joseph Siebert had only requested her because he didn't want the male instructors to see that he wasn't as good a skier as he claimed. Marie-Laure was used to men with a high opinion of themselves. Didn't she have three older brothers after all? Her brothers' teasing, mockery and put-downs had always provoked a reaction in the pit of her stomach, a fiery ball of determination not to be beaten. Monsieur Siebert, Jean-Luc and his fellow instructors all provoked the same feeling and a silent vow in her head: *This job is my way out and I'm not going to let you stop me.*

Boys always had to be told they were the best, she knew, otherwise they had a tendency to sulk. Each one of her brothers was somehow their mother's favourite. 'There's nothing better than my boys,' Mam had always said. 'I know they'll look after me.' She had carried on saying that, even when it was painfully untrue. Still, one of the brothers was still at home, Marie-Laure reflected, looking after Mam, which was more than she was doing herself. The daily guilt about leaving Dublin twanged in her mind.

It was unfortunate that the previous day's lesson with God's Gift to Women had not gone well. He'd refused to admit to his inexperience and wouldn't listen to her teaching; in fact, he had trouble acknowledging that he was the pupil and she the tutor. She had feared he might call a halt to the classes and she would lose the 200 francs, so she had reined in her advice, to bolster his pride and keep him sweet. *Just like any silly girl,* she told herself. She had given him the illusion that he was a better skier than he was, and now he had headed off alone. She knew that he would have seen himself emerging triumphantly onto the nursery slope, executing a few expert turns, before swooshing to a stop in front of her.

But if that was his plan, he should have been basking in her admiration an hour ago.

Climbing the next hairpin bend, she could see something lying across the road at the corner ahead. Something straight: a ski. Cold fear suddenly made her feel nauseous There was bound to be trouble now. The fool had got stinking drunk and had probably crashed into a tree: just the thing to happen on this icy path.

She began to run. 'I'm coming,' she called. No reply. Either he'd knocked himself out or was weak with pain from a broken leg.

She could see him now, lying on his back, among the pines at the side of the road. As she got closer, she thought how awkwardly he was lying – how uncomfortable he looked. Before she reached him, she knew. She had seen a dead person before.

Marie-Laure put her skis down and looked at him. A Hail Mary ran automatically through her mind.

The bastard. What kind of idiot skis into a tree and breaks his neck on a sunny morning?

He was lying with his legs half on the road, one ski still on, his body under the trees. She clambered through the deep snow to his head. And stopped.

It was not a broken neck that had killed him. He lay in a halo of blood, puddles of red staining the white all around him. Even the fallen pine cones were red. One of his bamboo ski poles had been driven through his throat.

Chapter 2

She found herself leaning against a tree trunk. A broken twig was sticking into the back of her neck. The man was dead. Her mother's voice wailed in her head: *This is all your fault, all your fault! Why did you let him do it Mary Dolores? Why didn't you stop him girl?*

She took a deep breath and focussed her brain so she could think rationally. How could such an appalling thing have happened? He must have failed to take the bend. Drunk maybe? Maybe not? Perhaps just going too fast? He must have put out a hand to protect himself, the pole hit a tree and was forced into his neck, piercing an artery….

Except that it was the sharp end, not the handle, in his throat. Maybe it happened as he fell? She stepped round his body and looked at the snow. There were no signs of a tumble; he seemed to have simply skidded. His other ski pole was hanging from his wrist, attached by the strap, as she had shown him.

Anxious to understand, she followed his traces a little way up the hill. They were not easy to see as the snow cover on the road was thin. There appeared to be the tracks of several skiers. Of course, Jean-Luc and his pupils had passed this way before Monsieur Siebert. However, she could see Siebert's tracks, just as they veered off at the bend. Beside them was a patch of trampled snow, as if someone had been waiting there. *As if,* she thought, *someone had been in his path, forcing him to swerve to avoid them.*

Or were they her own footprints? She checked – no. But perhaps someone else had been there and seen the body. If so, why had they not raised the alarm? Or perhaps they had. Perhaps a lone skier had come by, seen the disaster, realised there was nothing they could do and had carried on down to the *Café des Sports*, arriving after she had left.

'Marie-Laure!' She turned: two people were coming up the

road. It was Jean-Luc and Harald.

She tried to shout but found herself unable to make a noise. They broke into a run. 'Don't worry,' called Harald. 'Jean-Luc thought you might need help with the guy…' But then they reached her and saw what she was looking at.

'Shit,' said Jean-Luc. He struggled knee-deep into the snow to reach Siebert. 'Shit,' he said again, when he saw the blood.

Harald put his hand on her shoulder. For him, it was a big gesture of kindness and it was the worst thing he could have done. An urge to burst into tears swelled inside her.

'Come on,' he said. 'Put your skis on.'

*****

Marie-Laure sat on a hard wooden chair and stared at the snow outside the cafe. She could see Harald and Jean-Luc setting off up the road with the big sledge, normally used for hauling deliveries.

The lunchtime chef, Nathalie Lazare, placed a brandy on the table in front of her.

Marie-Laure had been pleased and relieved to find, when she got back to the café, that the one person she most wanted to see was already there – Nathalie, her friend and landlady. She had been a lodger at Nathalie's apartment for the past 18 months; only the previous evening they had been laughing about God's Gift to Women and his pompous airs. Nathalie came in on weekday mornings, to prepare the lunches, and her cooking was gaining the *Café des Sports* a good reputation.

'So who was this Siebert fellow?' she asked. 'Was he here on holiday?'

'He told me he worked for a family who are staying at the Hôtel Splendide in Chamonix. Somehow he'd convinced his boss that he needed to brush up on his skiing. He told me,

"You never know when it might be useful. Speed is all important in my job." He had a fast sports car too.'

Nathalie grimaced. 'Well, it looks like speed was the death of him. What was his job, exactly?'

'He said he was in 'security'.'

'Did he mean he was a bodyguard?' Then asked, 'What does his boss do then? Is he rich?'

'Must be if he's staying at the Splendide. Monsieur Siebert just said he had interests here. He's a Monsieur Andlau.'

'Sounds a bit German.'

'They're from Strasbourg. That's France isn't it?'

'It's been France since the end of the war,' Nathalie said firmly.

At that moment they heard the roar of a powerful car engine, which quietened to a low purr, before stopping. The front door opened and a man came into the bar. He looked around 50, dark haired, trim, wearing a full length camel-hair car coat which, to Marie-Laure, looked wonderfully decadent – warm and soft.

The man raised his hat. 'Good day. I'm looking for the lady skiing instructor. I was told I'd find her here.'

Marie-Laure stood up. 'Monsieur Andlau?' He nodded. She took a deep breath but even so the words came out strangely: 'I have to tell you some bad news…'

He broke in: 'Mademoiselle, you have a pupil, a Monsieur Siebert. I need to speak with him. It's urgent.'

'The bad news concerns Monsieur Siebert…' Her mind was whirling but she felt she had a responsibility to tell him. 'He's had an accident.'

'I must talk to him.'

'A really bad… I mean he's dead.'

Monsieur Andlau closed his eyes. He looked like a man who had received the news he'd been dreading.

'Have a seat,' said Nathalie. 'Would you like a brandy?'

Monsieur Andlau didn't seem to hear her. He opened his eyes and gazed so intently at Marie-Laure that her face began to flush.

'Where is he?' he asked.

'I found him on the road down from the P'tit Alpe. They've gone to fetch the… fetch him.'

'Mademoiselle – you found him?' Monsieur Andlau now appeared shocked.

'Yes. I went to look for him when he was late for his lesson.'

'But, how terrible for you.' Suddenly he seemed more concerned about her than his employee.

Nathalie put a glass of brandy on the table. He didn't touch it but sat down and Marie-Laure sat too. He leaned in towards her, so close she could smell his eau de cologne. 'How did he die?'

'He had some sort of collision and… got stabbed in the neck by his ski pole…'

'Was it an accident?' When she hesitated he asked, 'In your opinion mademoiselle? Tell me, I know nothing about skiing. Please. Could someone else have been involved?'

'There were marks in the snow – footprints. I think someone….' She realised what she was about to say and fell silent.

He nodded, as if this were confirmation.

She looked down at her hands. 'I'm sorry. I should not have let him go out alone. He was inexperienced.'

'Siebert had more than enough experience,' Monsieur Andlau said curtly. 'Have the police been called?'

Marie-Laure realised she didn't know. She called across to Nathalie behind the bar. 'Did anyone telephone the gendarmes?'

'Yes, as soon as we heard.' She looked towards the doors. 'I would've thought they'd be here by now.'

Monsieur Andlau murmured, 'Have you told anyone you don't think it was an accident?'

'I'm not saying it was not an accident,' Marie-Laure replied carefully.

'Indeed. Please, mademoiselle, I cannot tell you what to say, but I should be very grateful if you would not mention to the gendarmes or anyone the... possibility that it might not have been an accident.'

'It doesn't really matter what I think. They will ask Monsieur Sigurssen the questions. He's the boss. He knows what an accident looks like.'

'Of course. I am grateful to you mademoiselle.' Monsieur Andlau reached inside his coat and drew out a wallet. 'What is your fee for a lesson?'

'Two hundred francs.'

He counted out 12 one-hundred franc notes. 'I will pay you for six lessons for Monsieur Siebert.'

Marie-Laure was appalled. 'Of course not. I should have...'

'I beg you, you are not at fault here. Siebert was an adult, but he could also be a fool. He should have been able to look after himself.' He paused. 'Can you look after yourself mademoiselle?'

'Yes,' she said. What an odd question that was. He sighed and she thought there was fear in his face. His eyes were red-rimmed through lack of sleep. 'Are you alright monsieur?' she asked.

'It is not myself I worry about,' he replied, almost inaudibly.

There were shouts outside. Jean-Luc and Harald were bringing down the sledge, with its burden. At the same time, they heard the bell of the police van.

Monsieur Andlau buttoned up his coat. 'I must deal with poor Joseph and the gendarmes,' he said. 'Don't worry mademoiselle. I will ensure they don't make life difficult for you.'

Marie-Laure shook her head. 'I think they will.'

'I am a rich man. You'd be surprised at what I can do.'

Marie-Laure watched as he walked out on to the snow, slipping in his expensive shoes with their smooth, leather soles.

Nathalie came out from behind the bar as soon as he had gone. 'He didn't seem very upset.'

'Monsieur Siebert was an employee I suppose, not a member of his family.'

Outside there was the sound of another motor: an ambulance had arrived. People were moving around. Nathalie went to take a look. The men in tweed came into the café and hurried out again; Raymond and Pierrot must have returned with their morning's class.

Yet no-one came to ask for her, and as the stress caught up with her she suddenly felt very tired.

She could not believe that everything had gone so badly wrong. A few days ago she had been jubilant. She was a ski instructor, embarking on the life of adventure she had always dreamed of. Best yet, she'd finally said goodbye to the years of school teaching.

The transformation in her life had all happened within a few weeks and it was thanks to Claudine Lemaire. Six feet tall, athletically slim, and with a wonderfully self-confident disposition, she was always known as Claude. 'Claudine is the ghastly girl in Colette's novels,' she told Marie-Laure. 'What was my mother thinking of?' When Marie-Laure had arrived at the Sainte Thérèse Academy three and a half years before, she was the games teacher, and had taken Marie-Laure under her wing. They were the same age and Marie-Laure was in awe of everything about Claude: her elegance, her rebellious humour, her sporting prowess. Claude was nothing like the games teachers Marie-Laure had known from her schooldays. Grim-faced women bent on their mysterious purpose of increasing their pupils' suffering on this earth. Claude was joyous and enthusiastic and taught the schoolgirls to have fun. She had medals in swimming, athletics and – best of all – skiing.

Marie-Laure remembered the date – 15th November 1927, a Thursday she would never forget – when she had woken up to the first heavy snowfall she had ever seen. She had watched entranced as Claude went out to a steep field behind the kitchens and skied down. It looked so wonderful: she begged Claude to teach her. That first winter, she was a worse pupil than the youngest children but Claude was patient and gradually she could complete a slope without falling. A morning of fresh snow became her dream.

She had tried to describe the experience in letters to her mother. *It was a struggle to begin with but now it's the best fun I've ever had,* she'd written. Yet *fun* didn't really capture the exhilarating sense of freedom she felt on the slopes.

Mam had replied with her usual suspicion of all things new: *I don't like the sound of it at all. You're bound to catch your death.*

Then at the beginning of this season, back in December,

Claude had taken lessons with Harald Sigurssen. 'He's the best skier in Chamonix,' Claude had said. 'He's got no end of medals.'

Marie-Laure thought Claude was the best skier in Chamonix. 'You've got medals,' she pointed out.

'Only for the women's events. They're rubbish. We're only allowed to race over three kilometres.'

'Three kilometres would be enough for me.'

Everything seemed to have worked out so well for them all. Under Harald's tuition, Claude won more races. She reported that the cook was leaving the *Café des Sports* and it was just the work Nathalie was looking for. Then Claude's Christmas present to Marie-Laure was a lesson with the legendary Harald.

Initially Marie-Laure had been terrified of him. But he was a marvellous teacher and surprisingly encouraging. 'Claude has taught you well so far,' he said. 'But then you English women are keen learners.'

'I'm not English,' Marie-Laure said.

'French women should forget about their fashions and get on skis. It would do them the world of good,' he went on. 'In Norway all the women ski. It's healthy.'

At the end of the lesson he set up a slalom course on the slope in front of the café and watched as she came down it. 'You can turn without falling. It's good, but turns are not important. Don't be taken in by this new craze for downhill skiing. That's for the kind of brainless young men who like the thrill of speed. Going up a slope again and again and throwing yourself down it faster and faster is not skiing. Where is the joy of being in the mountains? The pleasure of feeling your skis carve fresh tracks through the trees...'

He went misty-eyed and she knew the lesson was over.

The next day she had been out on the nursery slope, practising by herself, when Harald came out with a young woman. Despite her pretty face and chic, fur-trimmed outfit, it was obvious that the woman wasn't happy. She crouched stiffly, crossing her ski tips and falling frequently. Harald did not shout at her and he helped her up every time she fell, but it was clear from his curt instructions and the bored tone in his voice that he thought his pupil was incapable of learning to ski.

At the end of the lesson, Harald had gone immediately into the bar to have a glass of beer. The woman had plonked herself down in a chair on the terrace, too exhausted to take her skis off, her furs wet and bedraggled. Marie-Laure approached her.

'Finding it hard?'

'Impossible,' muttered the woman. Tears were running down her cheeks. 'My husband's right. I've no co-ordination. I'm a hopeless case.'

'No-one's hopeless,' Marie-Laure said firmly.

'I am. I've never been sporty.'

'Me neither. Let me get you a cup of chocolate and then why don't you have a little practice with me?'

So she had spent half an hour with the woman – Geneviève – trying to show her what Claude had taught her and trying to remember how she, always a 'poor athlete' on her school report, had learned. After an hour, Geneviève was making her way down the slope, slowly but upright and without whimpering, even making a few careful turns.

Marie-Laure joined her at the bottom where Geneviève, flushed and triumphant, was talking excitedly to a sleek young man who was presumably the husband. Harald stood beside him. The husband peeled off a generous number of hundred-franc notes from a large billfold and gave them to Harald.

'You and your assistant have done wonders with my wife. She's such a little ninny,' he said. 'Same time tomorrow?'

Harald smiled. 'Why not.'

Back in the bar, Harald had given Marie-Laure the extra francs which the man had paid.

'If you want to take the lesson, same time tomorrow, you can have the whole payment.'

So Marie-Laure's career as a ski instructor had begun.

Two days before the new school term started in January, she went to see Reverend Mother at the Academy of Sainte Thérèse de la Petite Fleur, took her life in her hands and gave in her notice as English and German teacher, with apologies but with immediate effect.

She had never thought it would be easy. She wouldn't earn as much and there was no guarantee that there would be a steady stream of pupils. Now that the railway line from Paris was bringing in visitors keen to try to fashionable winter sports, ski schools were springing up all over the area. On the other hand, few were run by anyone with Harald's reputation and with his backing she felt she could make a go of it, even if she used up all her savings.

But she'd never imagined such a disaster as the death of a client. She longed to talk to Harald and be steadied by his fierce common sense.

Outside, cars drove off, one after another. Then there was silence for a while before a blast of cold air rushed into the café as the door opened. Harald entered, followed by Raymond, Jean-Luc and Pierrot.

Marie-Laure was aware that they were all looking at her. Harald was grim-faced; Jean-Luc had a curiously shifty look;

Raymond and Pierrot were smirking. Raymond went to the bar and poured himself a drink.

'You should go home Marie-Laure,' said Harald.

'Yes. I will.' She put on her coat and hat. At the door Harald came up to her. 'You don't need to come in tomorrow,' he said, awkwardness in his voice.

'I'll be alright.'

He cleared his throat. 'I mean you don't need to come in again. I think you'll agree… It was my mistake, to employ someone lacking in experience…'

Marie-Laure went cold. 'You're sacking me?' she asked.

She wanted to protest but hated the idea that it would sound like begging. What could she say? That it wasn't her fault? She could not bring herself to speak the words.

'This… accident will be the ruin of my school unless I take action…' Harald mumbled.

'But…'

'Be reasonable Marie-Laure…'

'Have the police threatened…?' she began. Perhaps rich Monsieur Andlau had not managed to fix things.

'Not the police, it's the Alpine Mountaineering Association!' Harald said. 'You know they've never approved of me and they will seize any excuse to have me closed down. I can't afford to tolerate negligence.'

'I see,' she said.

'We have professional standards to maintain. It's important if skiing is to develop as a sport with international credibility.'

'Quite right,' said Raymond at the bar. Pierrot nodded in self-righteous agreement.

She looked for Jean-Luc. Had he spoken up for her? But he was gazing purposefully out of the window, refusing to meet her eye. Maybe he was glad to be rid of her.

Raymond raised a glass. 'Goodbye Marie-Laure', he called. 'Delighted to have met you. Now fuck off back to your girls' school.'

Chapter 3

'Would it be so bad, going back to teaching?' Nathalie had returned to the apartment a little after Marie-Laure, and they sat opposite each other at the ancient kitchen table.

Marie-Laure slumped in despair. 'The last thing I want is to crawl to Reverend Mother and ask for my job back.'

'True, it would be a bit embarrassing. But she didn't want you to leave in the first place.'

'I don't care about being embarrassed. But I've spent twenty years of my life in one convent school or another. How did that happen? I've never wanted to be a nun. Not even when I was nine and all the other little girls fell in love with God for a few months and vowed to take the veil.'

Nathalie reached out and put her hand over Marie-Laure's. 'No-one's saying you have to be a nun. You can walk out of Sainte Thérèse and come back here at the end of the day and drink a whole bottle of wine if you want.'

'You're right but… teaching skiing was so much more fun than teaching English and I really thought I'd be able to earn some decent money.'

'Only in the winter. And anyway this craze for skiing might be finished come next year.'

Marie-Laure couldn't explain why she had felt driven to leave Sainte Thérèse, in pursuit of a life of freedom and adventure. What did that mean anyway? It seemed callous to talk about freedom when Nathalie, a widow at 33 with five small children, had little chance of finding any freedom herself.

The events of the day had only confirmed Nathalie's belief that skiing was a foolish pastime, bound to end in disaster. Marie-Laure recognised that Nathalie had been very restrained on hearing that her lodger was going to give up a steady job and throw herself down a mountain instead. And she was grateful that her promise to pay the rent without fail had been accepted without a murmur.

For Marie-Laure, lodging with Nathalie Lazare on the rue des Cavaliers, in the centre of Chamonix, was nothing less than a glorious haven, albeit a noisy one. Nathalie's husband Emile had died three years before and had left her with a large apartment on the second floor. He also left her with no money and no easy means of earning any, other than what dressmaking work she could find. The lunchtime job at the *Café des Sports* was a welcome supplement, but she was having to pay one of the neighbours to mind the youngest, four-year-old Charlot, during those hours. She charged Marie-Laure a small rent for a generously sized room and good meals, and in return Marie-Laure helped with the children and the cleaning, and stood particularly still while Nathalie held up dress patterns against her.

Marie-Laure had first come to the Sainte Thérèse in the summer of 1927, equipped with nothing more than her school French, which had been praised in Ireland but which immediately proved inadequate in France. Plus she had a letter of recommendation from the convent's sister-school in Blackrock, where she had taught English for four years. To begin with, the obvious arrangement was for her to lodge with the nuns. But that had been an uncomfortable time. She felt as if she were just another boarding school pupil, forever under the eye of the headmistress. Yet it also gave her the stability and peace she needed. Reverend Mother seemed to know that and asked her little about her background. But then again, perhaps Mother Anthony at Blackrock had already told her about Marie-Laure's stricken family. Nuns, it seemed, really did know everything.

Then one morning she'd dreamt that when she arose, instead of her own clothes on the chair beside her bed, there was a nun's grey shift, black gown and veil. Time to move out.

Claude, via her mother – who also knew everything – had heard that Nathalie was looking for a lodger. Marie-Laure was charmed by Nathalie's home, in a big 19th century building beside the river Arve. The faded pink shutters and wrought iron railings on the balconies seemed to her the epitome of Frenchness.

Living in the town meant an early morning bus ride up to the school, which was perched at La Platière, two kilometres along a winding road rising out of Chamonix. But the extra effort was worth it. Marie-Laure hit it off with Nathalie straight away; the large family reminded her of her own childhood in Churchtown, and she felt she was rejoining the real world. In fact it was a better world than the one she had left behind in Ireland, she told herself.

But, right now, sitting in the kitchen, Marie-Laure wasn't sure if she wanted to cry or rage. When she had left the *Café des Sports* that morning, jobless, she had walked the five kilometres back to Chamonix in a daze. The idea that the death was no accident niggled in her mind; something was not right and she hadn't been allowed to say so. But she couldn't hold any thought before it was swamped by a surge of anger and bitterness. She wanted to go to the top of Mont Blanc and yell 'It's not fair!' until her protest echoed in the ravines and made the glaciers growl.

By the time she'd reached the town centre, she found she was intensely tired, so bought some sugar-topped brioche buns at the patisserie to cheer herself up. She looked at them now on the table. They seemed rather small and not up to the task. She left the brioches to Charlot, went to her room and lay on the bed, her mind still bubbling with resentment.

When she woke it was already dark. From outside came the noise of a powerful motor. For a horrible second, she thought it was Monsieur Andlau again, come to accuse her. But no, pulling up in front of the building was a familiar automobile – a low, sporty, bright red Alfa Romeo 8C hard top, driven by the equally flamboyant Claude Lemaire. Marie-Laure went down to let her in.

Wearing a Madeleine Vionnet bias cut creation that flattered her slim figure, Claude stepped out of the car, chandelier drop earrings flashing under her short blonde hair as she zoomed into the kitchen.

Nathalie admired her outfit. 'A trouser suit looks so good on you. I wouldn't dare to wear one, but on you…'

Claude grinned. 'Trousers are so liberating, Nathalie. All your customers will be wanting them soon.' Then, to Marie-Laure, she said, 'Go and get changed! We're going to a party.'

'I've got nothing to celebrate.'

'Oh don't be such a misery!'

'But my pupil's dead and I've lost my job.'

Claude tilted her head a little to one side.

'It's true,' said Nathalie.

Marie-Laure tried to explain what had happened, yet it all

came out in such a confused rush that Claude stopped her. 'You need a drink,' she pronounced. 'And I know where to get one. Put something presentable on and come with me.'

Within minutes Marie-Laure had changed into a dove grey gown and dancing shoes, and was in the passenger seat of the Alfa. 'Right,' Claude said, revving the engine. 'Hôtel Splendide, here we come.'

Before Marie-Laure could protest, they were already on their way.

*****

It was obvious to Marie-Laure, that the Annual Reception of the Ski Club of the Haute Savoie was not the place for her to be.

The only thing that persuaded her to follow Claude into the ballroom of the Splendide was that she felt confident Harald Sigurssen would not be there. Though Vice President of the Ski Club of the Haute Savoie, he hated parties, and would definitely be in no mood for socialising this evening. She scanned the room: there was no sign of him, nor of Jean-Luc and his cronies, though, as instructors, they had probably not been invited.

Reluctantly, she followed Claude into the melée. The ballroom was packed with men and women, mostly young, sporty and fashionably dressed. They were the downhill crowd, the new skiers that Harald disapproved of. They, however, idolised him – or, more precisely, his medals – and his name as Vice President gave credibility to the Ski Club. Formed five years before, it was regarded by others in the town as a jumped-up clique of wealthy parvenues. The Ski Club's main function was to organise a programme of races: the downhill crowd lived for thrills and adored competition.

She recognised the Ski Club's new President, Dominic Peyrefitte. He was in his 40s, handsome, athletic and from the way he dressed, obviously rich. The money, though, came from his heiress wife. The couple were from Lyon, had moved to Chamonix a few years before and had been steadily buying up properties and land in the area. Harald despised them both, but led by Peyrefitte's dynamism and charisma, the Ski Club had doubled in size and winter tourism in the town was growing every year. The Peyrefittes were the darlings of the hotel owners and supported by the Mayor – who happened, by coincidence, to be a local hotel owner.

Traipsing behind Claude, Marie-Laure passed Monsieur Peyrefitte, who looked straight through her. Fortunately he had no idea she worked for Harald. Used to work for Harald. Used to be one of Harald's instructors until her pupil had died that morning with a ski pole through the throat.

She shivered. Had she heard a wisp of conversation? 'In a pool of blood… some German…' Was she imagining things?

She really needed to talk to Claude, but people were gathering round her friend: everyone wanted to hear about the races she had won in January.

'For God's sake, get me a drink,' Claude hissed to her.

At the temporary bar, Marie-Laure knew she was not imagining things. A loud voice broke out of the hubbub of conversation behind her: '… at Harald Sigurssen's school… right through the neck, can you imagine! Apparently he'd been drinking all morning…'

The story was doing the rounds. Marie-Laure noticed that people latched on to the idea that Monsieur Siebert was drunk. They didn't want to think that this was the sort of thing which could happen to anyone.

She took a glass of champagne to Claude, who was talking intently about race-start technique, then she wandered away again, feeling out of place and slightly too warm in her evening gown.

In an effort to cool herself she wandered out into the foyer. As she moved towards the reception desk a couple were coming down the stairs and, to her horror, she recognised the man.

He wouldn't want to acknowledge me here, surely?

However, he approached and nodded slightly.

'Mademoiselle.'

'Monsieur Andlau.' She did her best not to sound flustered.

'May I present my wife? Berthe, this is Mademoiselle… Monaghan, is that right?' He pronounced it with a hard G, as did everyone she met in France; she had become used to it.

Madame Andlau was a slim, upright woman in her 40s, impeccably but soberly dressed in a brown suit, her hair up in an old-fashioned chignon. She looked drawn and anxious.

'Are you visiting someone?' Monsieur Andlau asked.

'No, I came with a friend who is at the, er, Ski Club reception.'

She had not wanted to say the word 'ski'. Madame Andlau stiffened and looked down. But Monsieur Andlau spoke smoothly.

'We are going there ourselves. We've been invited by a Monsieur Parfaite… Peyrefitte? I'm not sure if he knows who we are…'

Marie-Laure nodded. 'He'll know. It's a small town. I expect he wants to offer condolences and… reassure you.'

'We are not intending to make any fuss!' Madame Andlau said sharply.

Marie-Laure nodded again. 'They don't want it to be thought that skiing is a dangerous sport. Well, they sort of do… but they don't…'

'Skiing is so ridiculous,' another voice broke in. A young woman had come to join them.

'This is our daughter Rosa,' Madame Andlau said.

Marie-Laure tried not to stare. Rosa was about 20, she guessed, and strikingly beautiful. Tall, with the sort of blue eyes and wheat-gold hair Marie-Laure had never seen before in real life, Rosa seemed to have stepped out of a Rhineland fairy tale.

To cover her embarrassment, Marie-Laure asked, 'Do you prefer other winter sports Mademoiselle?'

'Certainly not. Such physical activity would be improper for a woman in my position. I am engaged to be married you know.' Her reply was emotionless and cold.

There was a second awkward silence, then Marie-Laure murmured, 'Congratulations.'

The three of them then moved into the ballroom and were almost immediately swept away by Monsieur Peyrefitte. Marie-Laure could sense a hum of suppressed gossip, while at the same time the eyes of the men in the room were being drawn ineluctably to Rosa.

She went to find Claude. 'The man who died – his boss is here,' she said quietly.

'Oh. I expect you're not his favourite person.'

'Actually he's being very nice to me. I don't know why.'

There was a sudden loud honk of laughter, as if a hungry donkey had been let into the room by mistake.

'Oh yes, and my mother's here as well,' said Claude. 'Come on.'

Claude's mother, the legendary Louise Lemaire, was

holding court in one corner of the room, using a half-full champagne bottle, representing herself, to re-enact her progress down a particularly tricky slope. She was surrounded by people Marie-Laure thought of as the skiing old guard. Weatherbeaten faces and an air of impatience at being inside four walls. They had been joined by some of the younger Ski Club members, who seemed both fascinated and appalled by this beetle-browed, box-shaped woman, with a voice like an alpenhorn.

'If I'd lost a ski there it would have fallen all the way to Argentières and I'd have had to run down on one ski to find it,' Louise continued. 'Not that I haven't done that before...'

'Madame Lemaire achieved so many exploits in her youth,' one of the old guard explained to a smooth-faced Parisian. 'She was winner of the first ever international women's ski race, here in Chamonix, twenty years ago.'

'Twenty-three. Seems like yesterday!' Louise hooted. 'Such a lot of fuss about that race. People disapproved because we crossed the finishing line sweaty and laughing! It wasn't considered ladylike.'

Marie-Laure thought of the lovely Rosa. She would never sweat.

'Believe me, my dear, you should have heard the objections when I started out,' Louise went on. 'Young ladies shouldn't ski! In my grandmother's day they said young ladies shouldn't ride bicycles and before that, shouldn't ride in steam trains. People seemed to think it made you lose your virginity!'

Marie-Laure contemplated Louise's virginity uneasily. The ski champion had no truck with men and Marie-Laure rather thought she had borne her daughter through some sort of Alpine parthenogenesis. Though the physical differences between the two women implied someone else had had a hand in Claude's conception. Well, not a hand, exactly…

'Mind the champagne mother,' said Claude. 'People are getting soaked.'

'Marie-Laure!' Louise greeted her with a kiss and took her aside, away from her audience. 'How's life with Harald?'

Marie-Laure hesitated. Louise was one of the few people in Chamonix whom Harald liked, and no doubt she would hear the story from him. Marie-Laure wanted to give Louise her account first and tease out why she felt the death was not an accident.

They went to a quiet corner and she told them all about Joseph Siebert – boastful drunkard, God's Gift to Women and her passport to a successful ski-instructing career. And then of his blood-soaked death. She told them how Monsieur Andlau had turned up, and how Harald had sacked her.

'My first real pupil. And he damn well gets killed,' she said, as lightly as she could to stop herself breaking into tears.

'So that's what everyone's talking about. I heard he was a German,' Louise said. 'It all sounds very odd. Tell me again what he looked like when you found him.'

Marie-Laure tried to remember every detail. Louise listened closely, asking a few questions.

'Huh,' she grunted. 'I've seen some skiing accidents in my time but I've never come across anyone getting a pole in the neck. It's as if someone murdered the chap and tried to make it look like an accident but didn't know what they were doing.'

Claude was impressed with the notion of murder. 'Could it be deliberate?' she asked.

'I did get the feeling, looking at the tracks, that Monsieur Siebert had encountered another person. But nobody saw anyone else,' Marie-Laure said. Plus, she now realised, her greatest sense there was something wrong about the death had come from Monsieur Andlau himself and the fear in his eyes.

'I dare say the gendarmes will get to the bottom of it,' Louise said.

Despair hit Marie-Laure again. 'Monsieur Siebert's employer doesn't want the police looking into this too closely and he'll make sure they don't,' she muttered.

Claude was indignant. 'So the whole affair is going to be classed as an accident, and you've lost your job for being negligent? We're not having that! Where is this man? He's got to report it properly!'

She looked angrily round the room for Monsieur Andlau and Marie-Laure was afraid she would stomp off and harangue him in front of the Ski Club committee.

'Stop, Claude! He's here with his wife and daughter. They must all be very upset – don't make it worse.'

'The point is,' Claude said, 'they'll probably be packing up and leaving tomorrow…'

'…With the body,' Louise added, helpfully.

'Er, with the body,' Claude went on. 'How do you transport a body? Anyway, they'll be gone and you'll be taking all the blame.'

'Harald will get the blame too,' Louise said. 'He won't like that. You must tell him it wasn't an accident. He probably already has a suspicion.'

'Harald will think I'm mad and then he definitely won't want me back.'

'This business won't sort itself out on its own,' Louise said firmly. 'I bet Peyrefitte has already got his claws into your Monsieur Andlau and is persuading him not to make a fuss.

The Ski Club is determined to have Chamonix the winter sports capital of the Alps. So of course, this Siebert will be painted as a drunken fool and you as an inexperienced nobody. Then everyone can forget about the unpleasantness and get back to bringing the hordes down from Paris and making as much money from them as possible.'

'If you really think it wasn't an accident, you've got to tell the authorities,' Claude said.

A wave of fear swept over Marie-Laure. 'But... no... they'll say it was my fault.'

'It wasn't your fault,' Claude stated. 'Just tell the police the facts.'

Marie-Laure knew that to Claude, facts were indisputable and the authorities were there to help.

But her memory jumped back to when she was a little girl, crouched unseen at the top of the stairs, hearing her brother's voice as he went out the door, on the last night of his life.

'Speak to the police, and we're dead.'

Ace of Clubs
Tiffany Lindfield

Saturday Afternoon
Tom

Tom McCann was one of those men who wore white pants with pink shirts, unbuttoned to show off gold chains. On his wrist he always wore expensive timepieces.

It was the 80's when women would turn their heads to get a better look; his body built with free weights. He showed it off then, and his tan, wearing short gym shorts, and wife beaters, even in cold weather.

The 80's were gone though. Been and gone. Washed over by the 90's, and the 90's were gone, too.

The girl at the Starbucks counter was cherry-lipped young, lips that didn't need chapstick to shine. "Can I help you, sir?" she asked with a name tag that read: *Kara*

He heard her say it, but he mostly tried to get a glance down her polo work shirt, disappointed that it wasn't low-cut. She licked her lips, and he felt a tickle in his groin. He leaned over the counter, flexing a sagging bicep. She looked at him with a mix of revulsion and annoyance. A young guy, another employee, stocking bakeries in the display case looked up to Tom, rolling his eyes.

*****

Kara

Tom handed her a card before walking off. Or strolled. It seemed to her that he strolled. And before leaving, he turned around to give her a wink.

Holding the card, she twitched her nose at the man's smell. He smelled like cigarettes which reminded her of home, and she hated home. He was a real estate developer, the card said. Scribbled on the back: *I Pay 5,000 for one night—Call Me. Must be 21 or over!*

She made a motion of disgust but kept the card, shoving it inside her apron pocket. *Five thousand dollars.* That could buy a car. That could get her away from home.

Saturday Evening

She thought a lot more about a car after Starbucks closed and she was sitting, shivering in the empty parking lot waiting for her mother to pick her up. She had forgotten her jacket earlier and so, sat huddled with her arms wrapped tightly around her chest, cussing a storm.

A stranger pulled up in a new Lexus, sleek black. It was a middle-aged woman. "Y'all' still open?" she asked, rolling down the window.

"No, ma'am. Closed an hour ago."

"Are you okay?"

Kara knew the woman had pulled up to help her. "Waiting on a ride that never came. And my cell died…."

"Where do you live?" The woman asked with pity in her

voice.

"Off Summer—near Highland Street."

"Get in the car. A young girl shouldn't be sitting in a dark lot alone. It's not safe. I'll take you home."

Kara got in the car, feeling the comfort of leather seats with electric warmers. The woman's car was cluttered with papers, pacifiers—she counted five on the floorboard alone. A diaper bag, and other mother essentials littered the car. Kara noted classical music playing low on the radio.

"I hope you don't mind me asking but who was supposed to pick you up?"

"My mom, but she's usually late. This time really late," Kara said casually, used to it.

"Wow...really so unsafe for a young woman to be waiting outside like that."

"No, but what else can I do?" Kara asked, tired, ready to be home, shower and then go to bed. School was early tomorrow, and she had a test she was determined to *ace*. This was her way out, she thought. Good grades. She could tell the woman was a do-gooder and wanted her to open up or something like the guidance counselor at school. But she had opened up to neighbors, police officers, social workers—you name it, and she was still stuck.

"My name's Sally. What about you, dear? What's your name?"

"Kara."

"Kara...that's a very unique name."

"So, you got a kid?" Kara blurted out.

"Three little princesses." The woman said with a smile. "Three little girls."

"Oh, damn. I bet you're super tired."

"Well...being a mom isn't easy, but I wouldn't trade it for the world," Sally said with another smile that seemed too simple for Kara.

"I guess that explains the pacifiers."

Sally laughed, a laugh that sounded innocent to Kara. "Well, that's my youngest. I think we have about a hundred pacifiers between home, work and school."

Silence.

Kara imagined being loved enough by someone to have multiples of anything, *100's* of anything she wanted. It seemed excessive, almost silly, but something she wished she'd had growing up. Though she was only sixteen, she didn't consider the fact that she still needed someone to love her. "Next street, turn right. That's my street."

"Is this it?"

Kara could see the worry in the woman's face. Kara knew the woman had always had someone to pick *her* up. And couldn't figure that some people really didn't have anyone that gave a good goddamn. "I appreciate the ride. I really do."

The woman dug in her purse for something. She pulled out a wallet. Kara thought she was going to hand her money, but she handed her a business card instead. Kara took it.

Sally's face went serious. "Look, this is my card. I work as an associate pastor of a small church. We have lots of youth programs for kids, teens, and things like that. You can reach me anytime—if you need help. If you need anything, call me...anytime."

Kara took the card looking closely at Sally. She looked so much like a Sally with plain features and small wrinkles around her eyes, and a pink headband holding back thin hair from a kind smile. "Thanks."

Kara went inside to see her mother passed out on the front sofa. *Probably Xanax.* Kara didn't bother waking her. Roaches scattered in the kitchen; a cat meowed. Kara grabbed a box of stale crackers and a coke. Sitting on her bed, she licked the salt off the crackers, then swallowed them down with the coke. She looked at the cards again, flipping them over, holding them side-by-side and then shoved them in her nightstand drawer. She turned out the light.

*****

Monday Lunchtime

Kara

"You really should start taking school more seriously," Kara said, picking at White Station's High School spaghetti special."

Candace grimaced. "I don't have brains like you."

"Okay but don't depend on me to take care of you in five years."

"Really," Candace said, standing up tall: she was the tallest girl in the school, the team captain of the girls' basketball team.

But Kara stopped her, asking her to stay. "Look, let's not fight."

Candace settled back into her seat.

"Like I said, I had a weird fucking night last night." Kara laid Tom's card on the table between two plastic trays of school lunch food. Candace straightened up, popping a peppermint in her mouth, picking up the card. "*Ghezz,* what a creeper."

"I know, right."

"I don't know, Kar."

Kara leaned in over her tray of food with black hair falling over mashed potatoes and uneaten spaghetti. She gently took Candace's face in her hand and kissed her on the cheek, then whispered in her ear, "It will be fun. The ultimate revenge against all the old pervs in America."

Candace pushed back. "Fun? Are you serious? You're talking about tying a grandpa up and robbing him. Not sure *fun* is the word that pops up in my head. More like a prison sentence."

Kara's pale face turned crimson as she spoke. "You really aren't joining the dots, are you? This old creeper is going to have money on him if we set up the arrangement, and we'll make him think we are all into whatever nasty shit he has planned. We will put on a show, tie his old ass up…make him think it's like a bondage thing and then rob his stupid ass. It really is that fucking simple and *boom* we are five thousand dollars richer—or more. You know these old timers keep banks under their mattresses. And our *ace,* the thing that guarantees us an out is even if he's dumb enough to go crying to the pigs, we will just show them this card. The pigs will see us as two innocent high school chicks—as victims."

Candace's bright blue eyes darted around, no make-up. '*I sweat too much for make-up,*' she had told Kara when they first started dating. And she did, being a star athlete. "Kara, I just don't know."

"You know I can make this happen. I will perfect every detail. There will be no room for error."

"I know," Candace said quietly.

Monday Evening

Jeremiah

Tom's brother, Jeremiah, found Tom at his usual spot, *Hooters*. It had become his tradition to pine away at the water hole since his wife left, taking their little boy to romp around Europe on his dime—with a man her own age, a man younger than Tom. Jeremiah snuck up from behind Tom, who sat poised at the bar eating a hoagie.

"Hey, buddy. Philly cheese?"

"Yep. I'll order you one."

"No. Kathy is cooking right now. I'm sure of it."

Tom stared at the TV screens above the bar.

"Did you go in for treatment today?"

Tom looked down, picked up a fry and ate it gingerly, staring blankly at the cheerleaders' seductive dance on the screen.

"Tom?"

"I ain't doing it. I told you that two months ago. You and Kathy jumped my ass, so I told you I'd give it another shot, and I did."

"So, you went?"

Tom looked at his younger brother. "Yeah, I went, and you know what I saw?

"No. I don't. What'd you see?" Jeremiah asked, kindly.

"I saw death run over. That's what and I ain't goddamn doin' it. I got a good year without treatment, maybe two with the chemo. But what the hell is two years when you are sucking poison into your veins? I'm gonna live my last goddamn year, poison free, doing what I want to do – like God intended for men to live."

"Is this what you call living, brother? Sitting at a bar every night, staring at a TV?"

"You come in here to crucify me?"

"No, I came here to tell—"

"—What the hell do you want me to do every night? Sit in that house all alone? Is that better than sitting here? At least here, I can listen to people talking, watch them laughing"— Tom began pointing to patrons in the bar, knocking a few fries off his plate—"What the fuck do I have at home?"

"How about thinking about your son, Tom? About getting him back home? Where he can be close to his family again? Where he can be close to you in your..."

"...Say it," Tom demanded but Jeremiah shook his head. "My last fucking days?" Tom went on, slurring his words. "Look. I miss my boy. I'd give anything to see him, but she ain't bringing him back. She's just waiting on me to die. Waiting on her big payday. That's why the bitch married me. For money."

"Yeah and why did you marry her? It wasn't love for you either. It was for sex. I mean, if we are to play the blame game, Tom."

"I don't blame her for a fucking thing. If I did, she'd be dead. You know I can have her killed." Tom snapped his fingers. "Like that."

Jeremiah took a deep breath, shaking his head. He hated his brother more than he loved him. He resented his stubbornness, but he also felt obligated to him—as his natural brother, and as his brother in Christ; Jeremiah tried to remember this obligation, pulling on the roots of his religion. "Kathy talked to Emma last night and she's willing to come back home. She's willing to bring Tobey back and stay here until...until the end. You need this time with your son. He's going to need it, too. He's going to need the memories with his father. You remember we didn't have that growing up."

Tom chuckled. "Kathy did that?"

"You know the power of Kathy," Jeremiah said with pride.

"Damn good woman. Hell of a diplomat or a lousy diplomat with a hell of a bargaining chip. What'd she promise that whore? All my goddamn money?"

"No. She promised her you would respect her and respect that you two are no longer together. That Emma can come and go as she pleases and that you will not try to control her." Jeremiah raised his voice as he saw Tom's face begin to redden in patches of anger. "Tom, and—

"—She ain't sleeping with that bus boy in my house!"

"It will be just her and Tobey. Do you want to see your son, Tom? Do you want this time with him, or do you want to die like this—without an ounce of grace?"

"Of course, I want to see him."

Jeremiah swung his body to face the bartender.

Tom finished off the hoagie sandwich in large, gross bites. He slugged his beer down. "When's she coming back?"

"Before the month is out. Kathy will make the arrangements."

Tom clumsily wiped his face. "Okay."

"When she gets here Tom, it's about you and Tobey. Anything between you and Emma is dead and gone."

"I know that, and you better believe if there's one thing this old man ain't gonna fuck up, it's that. I love that little boy. More than anything."

Jeremiah could see his brother's eyes tear up, the humanity in his brother's heart. "Okay."

Jeremiah stood up. "I gotta get back home to the fam."

Tom waved him off, but before Jeremiah could walk away, Tom turned to him. "Am I my brother's keeper?"

"You've been mine," Jeremiah answered, honestly. His brother, despite all his faults, and even the animosity between them had been there to help him when he needed it. Jeremiah saw his brother's eyes start to tear up again. Tom turned away. Jeremiah held his gaze on the slumped old man for a bit longer then walked out, passing a woman, sitting alone at the bar. She was blowing smoke rings in the air. Her eyes were a pitch dark and she stared at him, smirking. She mouthed the words, *'Boo,'* then smiled showing rows of rotted teeth.

Jeremiah turned from her look as a chill moved up his spine. At the bar door, he couldn't help but turn around to make sure Tom was still alive. Tom was sitting on the same stool, staring at the same TV. Jeremiah was struck by a surreal thought; the rowdiness of Tom's youth seemed all settled into an old man pacified with the *evils* of TV. Jeremiah shook his head.

✶✶✶✶✶

Tuesday Evening

Kara

Kara sat on her bed, two mattresses, one on top of the other, in the corner of her small room; the only clean spot in the house. She held Tom's card in her hand, the flicker of cheap candles scattering across its surface. The sounds of birds chirping in some faraway forest came from an old CD player she had stationed on her dresser. She wondered who had captured their voices, and what they were saying. She had learned from one of her Advanced Placement classes that birds chatter in the morning to establish territory. She figured she wasn't much different from them, locking the door of her room, the one space in the house she could control. She kept the room safe, clean, and quiet. A torn limb from the rest of the house, one rotting, her mother the poison.

She tapped a text to Tom:

> 5,000 really?

A quick response came:

> *Who is this?*

> Kara. Starbucks? Remember me?

> *I do.*

He didn't respond after that. Kara grew impatient staring at the phone, her eyes glazing over the empty screen. She stood up, walking out of the room, and past her mother sprawled on the sofa, passed out. Ramen noodles again. She poured hot water in one of the ramen cups, put it in the microwave, slamming the door loud, hoping it would jerk her mother awake. She opened a kitchen drawer, roaches scattering and dug out a plastic fork still in packaging. She refused to use any of the silverware in the house, always keeping a stash of plastic ware from her job.

Kara slurped the noodles, and the phone beeped. She picked her phone back up.

> *You want me?*

> I do ☺ But can't come alone. I want to bring my girlfriend.

> *Lesbian lovers?*

Kara cringed. It irked her how the boys and men took pleasure in her sex life with other females. Didn't they know real lesbians had no use for them? Sure, there were the wanna-be-lesbians who would kiss their friends at a party, but everyone knew it was for the sake of the male gaze. She hated those girls. And their parties. She loved females, knew it from the time she was a kid, even before puberty, and kissed them for pleasure, not crowd pleasing. And here she was, planning to do just that for the kicks of some grandpa; her stomach turned at the thought and she hated him for it.

"You got it coming, sicko," she said, typing a response.

> Yes. Is that O.K?

> *Fine but not paying double.*

Kara gritted her teeth.

> Did I ask you to pay extra?

> *You and her are at least 21?*

"Fuck," Kara said, then responded.

> Yep.

Call for details sweetheart.

Kara revisited the noodles, but they were soggy now. A deep sigh, she didn't want to call him. She knew she'd have to whisper loud like Marilyn Monroe or something close, stroking his perverse ego, but the money lured her. "You have no clue what's coming, sicko," she said, taking the cup of noodles to the kitchen, tossing them in the sink. Squatting outside on the house's driveway, she cleared her throat, practicing a sexy voice, then called him.

*****

Wednesday Afternoon

Tom

Tom called Mona, an old housekeeper, and the nanny Beatriz. He needed his house to be back in working order if his son were coming home. He had them stock the refrigerator with food; foods kids liked, and even Emma's favorite things to eat. He knew what they liked and wanted them to have it. It was the only way he knew how to show love. Buy things, to sit back and watch people unwrap whatever he'd bought them.

A pep came to his step; even his bad knees ached less. He ate dinner at home for the first time in months, and on this night, went swimming in his large indoor pool. He loved to swim, and he loved the thought of his son coming back home—his family—even if things weren't the same as before they left; before things went to shit between him and Emma.

Just as he was toweling off, the girl from Starbucks messaged him. He held the phone in his wet, pruned fingers.

He tapped fingers on the phone, his thumb getting in the way. Before it was said and done, the girl texted she would arrive that coming Friday night at 8:00 PM with some other girl, her girlfriend apparently. He didn't believe a bit of that, figuring the girl was just nervous and wanted a friend with her. Whatever, he would play along.

He chuckled to himself, with a lopsided smirk on his face. He didn't think she would even message, and now he wondered if she'd really show. She wouldn't regret it if she did, he thought, standing up to admire his own reflection on the surface of the pool. He still felt like he had it, having maintained a better physique than most other men his age. He knew how to please a woman. "I make 'em cum two or three times, every time," he said, chuckling.

*****

Thursday Evening

Candace

Kara had titled their adventure *Mission Easy*. Candace scoffed at this, digging in the back of her closet for something '*sexy.*' Given that she dressed like a boy most of the time, this wasn't an easy feat. In the back of her closet, she found yellow basketball shorts from two years back. She pulled them on. They were too short. "Is this what sexy is?"

She wouldn't be able to wear any of Kara's stuff either, because she was taller than Kara, thinner, too. "I'm a giraffe," she would say to describe herself. She picked up her landline phone, one shaped like Garfield the Cat. Every time she picked it up, she was reminded of the birthday her parents had given it to her. It was during her Garfield phase, when she used to write fanfic based on the comics.

Kara picked up.

"I can't find anything," Candace said, staring at her baseball bat legs in the floor length mirror – another gift from her parents.

"Thought you said you were going with an old skirt from the fairy costume."

"That was a thought," Candace said, staring at the small fairy dress from three years ago. "I've grown a lot since then."

Kara was thinking on the other end. Candace tapped her foot, hoping Kara would just call the whole crazy thing off. *Mission Easy Halted Due to Wardrobe Malfunction!*

"I'll find something of mine you can wear. Don't worry about it. Just get some sleep."

"Kar...I really don't want to do this. I don't know how to do any of this."

"This isn't easy for me, either. Just keep your eye on the prize. The money. I'll do all the legwork," – Kara laughed at this – "You just back me up."

"How are we getting there tomorrow? Is that figured out?" Candace asked, hoping not.

"My cousin Dusty is gonna take us. He promised to wait outside for us, too – down the street. We're safe. He'll keep his cell on and will watch for me to send him a safety code every thirty minutes. If it's more than one minute over the safety code time then he's calling the police."

"Kara – safety codes? If this is so quick and easy, we wouldn't need safety codes."

"It's just an extra layer of protection. Now stop worrying. I must plan this to the T so I don't have time to coddle you. You need to focus... Are you focused?"

"Yes. Kara," Candace said, guilt outweighing her bottling resentment. She didn't want to let Kara down.

"Dusty will pick me up from work Friday night and then we'll head to your house. We can stop at a gas station to change you into what I find."

Candace sat quiet on the phone letting Kara repeat the details a few more times, and then she hung up. She laid on her bed, feeling slivers of anxiety creep along her body. She couldn't take it and went downstairs, thinking maybe she could lounge in the sunroom. The downstairs was quiet, the family cat, Rebel, rested on a small dent he had made on the top of the couch over the course of many years. It was his spot.

Candace rubbed his face, feeling whiskers on her fingers. Everyone was cozy in the house, except for her. She knew her parents were asleep. She went into the sunroom and laid out on a soft daybed. A small lamp was on, and its soft glow calmed her, along with the moonlight seeping in from outside. She repeated the mantra, soothing herself: *Kara will keep us safe.*

*****

Friday Night

Kara

Dusty pulled up at Starbucks in a small two-door, close to an hour after it had closed. Kara wanted to get in the car and punch his lights out. She had imagined beating his face in – but she was at his mercy – so she got in the car with a glare, and a grin, tossing her backpack and sports bag onto the back seat. Dusty apologized saying it took Karen – Kara's aunt and his mother – longer than usual to go to sleep. He bragged to Kara about how he pulled the keys out of his mother's purse so slow that not even a mouse moved.

"Don't mind me," Kara said as she crawled in the backseat and began to change from her Starbucks uniform into a short black skirt, a halter top, and stripper boots, topping it off with red lipstick, as Dusty turned onto Candace's street. "Her parents rich?" he asked.

Kara pointed. "Both of them are math professors. The red brick house is hers."

And Candace was waiting. Kara laughed at her standing there in *Hello Kitty* pants and a sports tank.

"She's so fucking tall and skinny," Dusty said cringing.

"Shut up! She's my girl."

"Whatever," he said, bringing the car to a stop alongside the curb where Candace stood.

Candace got inside. "Whatever what?"

"Nothing, baby, get back here and put these on."

Candace looked at Dusty. "Hey Dusty," she said clumsily crawling into the backseat.

Candace

Kara handed her red boy shorts, a sequined top, and black heels.

Candace held the shoes up, knowing they would be too small for her large feet.

"It's what I got."

Candace held up the shorts and shirt. These were things she would never wear. Never ever wanted to wear. And the idea of putting them on and trying to prance around humiliated her in a nauseous way. She looked Kara over, envying how easy it was for her to take on the role of a sex kitten. Not only take it on, but also look good doing it. With the clothes on, she felt like a flamingo, long-legged and awkward. From the sports bag Kara dug out a small bottle of vodka, and pills, things she no doubt took from her mother. Kara used her teeth to break one of the pills in haphazard halves, giving Candace the larger half and the bottle. "Here, swallow it with a few gulps. It will take the edge off."

Kara went to pass Dusty the rest of the bottle and more pills. "Dusty the rest of this is yours but don't use any of it until after you drop us off back home. You're the driver. We need you to be sober as a church mouse."

"I can handle a few fucking pills."

"Dusty!"

"Okay. I got it. Damn."

"I'm serious about you waiting. Last thing we need is for you to be too fucked to help us if we need it."

"I said I got it, Kara. Now stop."

Kara sighed, leaning back, and her anxiety made Candace's anxiety worse. She kept looking at Kara's backpack, knowing what 'accessories' it contained. She wanted to scream for Dusty to stop the car. To let her out. She could run home on the terror in her heart. Kara took her hand and Candace could feel the sweat in Kara's palms. She kept swallowing, feeling like she might choke on her own heartbeat. She waited for the calm Kara had promised the Xanax would bring.

'Destination is on the Right,' the GPS said.

"Here," Dusty said, turning back to them with a twisted

grin and Candace thought of the absurdity of it all. A boy driving them as prey for another man – very much a predator.

Candace climbed out, followed by Kara, holding the backpack by its straps.

Kara

Tom opened the door wearing a red robe. It looked velvet, which seemed odd, Kara thought for a man to wear such a thing. "Hey ladies," he said, letting them in, leading them both inside a house unlike either of them had seen before. The entrance alone looked like it may be the size of her entire house, Kara thought.

"Wow!" Kara said, hearing the awe in her voice. Tom smiled at this, and Kara's smile slipped into a sardonic smirk.

He led them to a large room with a bar, bar stools included, a fine pool table, and behind a thick curtain was a miniature movie theatre. He went straight to the bar, making drinks. "Y'all old enough to drink?" he asked with a laugh, then, "sit down lovelies."

They sat side by side at the bar, Kara dropping the backpack between her feet. To Kara, Candace looked like a small mouse with large eyes, eyes that nervously scanned the room. Tom's robe was open in the front revealing a body, once chiseled, now flabby with wrinkled skin, dotted with gray hair. He had a tattoo on his forearm. It looked like something Kara had seen before but couldn't quite place.

"What's the tattoo?" she asked, hearing a tinge of uneasiness in her voice, which angered her. She needed him to be under her absolute control, and her voice needed to demand that.

"Air Force darlin.' You lookin' at a man born and bred in the military. Screwdrivers," he said, handing them each a drink.

Kara noted that he was eyeing Candace hard. "Kara told me you were a doll, but you aren't. You're a living angel."

Candace looked down with cheeks the color of spilled blood. Tom came around the bar with a drink in his hand and slid it on the bar after a swig. He stood behind Candace and spun her stool to face him. Kara watched, hawk-eyed on her mouse.

"Stand up for a minute, darling."

Candace looked at Kara who gave her a reluctant nudge of approval. This asshole wasn't playing by the rules, Kara thought. He was making moves too fast. "So, Tom, let's start with the show we've been talking about. Let's get warmed up first."

He ignored her as he sized up Candace like an art piece. Kara could see Candace turn away from his face with the look of pure grade A disgust. "You got the legs, the figure of a runway model, you know that?"

"No. No one has ever told me that," Candace sputtered out, humbly, honestly.

"Tall. Long-legged, slim-waisted angel," he said, moving his hand to touch her cheek.

Kara looked on as Candace's eyes began to well with tears. An odd twinge of jealousy hit her in the stomach. He hadn't noticed her at all, which was strange. She was always noticed by men. Kara took a drink, watching Candace scoot back from his touch, then sitting and sliding as far back as she could on the bar stool.

"So, who's the man in the relationship?" He asked as if anything was funny.

Kara stood up. "She's uncomfortable. Please. I told you from the start that you couldn't touch her."

Tom turned to Kara, chuckling. "You must be the one who wears the pants."

Kara swallowed hard, as if gulping down boiling water.

"Look. Relax a little," he said, spreading his hands out. "I just want to give her a small kiss on the cheek."

Kara took a deep sigh as Tom leaned into Candace's crying face, pinning her against the bar. "You're a real virgin? Aren't you?"

Kara's stomach went sick. The look of fear on Candace's face killed her. She yanked the small backpack up into her lap, pulling out a .22 caliber pistol from one of the side pockets. Off the stool, she move behind Tom who remained oblivious, running his fingers through Candace's hair, petting her like she was a toy.

Kara held the gun straight out, not the slightest tremble in her hands. Only rage. Pure, unfiltered rage. "Get the fuck off her now!"

Tom turned around nonchalantly. Candace bolted up, sliding to the end of the bar. "Oh my God! Oh my God!"

Kara motioned for Candace, keeping the gun steady in Tom's face. "Get the fuck behind me Candace. Tom, you sit the fuck down. Sit the fuck down with your hands up, over your ugly head."

Tom sat down, his hands up. "Sweetheart, put the gun down."

Kara turned her head back for a brief second, catching a glimpse of Candace behind her, shaking. "Get the rope out of the bag, Candace."

Candace in heavy sobs picked up the small backpack resting by Kara's feet, pulling out rope.

"Candace buck up! Go over there and tie up his arms and legs. Arms first. Tom if you make one move, I'll put a bullet in your head."

Candace looked like a wounded child, holding the rope, her whole body shaking. "Kar?"

"Tie him up, Candace! Now!"

Candace lips trembled. "He'll grab me. I can't."

"If he so much as blinks, I'll shoot him. Now get over there! Tom put your hands straight out"

Candace in a full ugly cry began to tie his arms as Kara continued to hold the gun to his face. Candace then tied his feet, backing up quickly when done. Kara drew closer to him, the gun inches from his face. "New plan, motherfucker. You give us the money and you live to see another day. Actually, make it twenty thousand for the trouble."

Tom laughed a hearty laugh. "That's what you want—the money?" Go ahead and kill me darling. You ain't getting a penny without working for it."

"Kara!" Candace screamed and Kara knew Candace was begging for them to go home, to just leave, to go home and play music off YouTube, anything but this. And the plea made Kara's anger rise higher, hitting the ceiling. She hated people who didn't have the grit to survive. Kara's face was twisted in soft folds of hot rage. "Get a grip. I can't baby you and get what we need at the same time."

Kara turned back to Tom. "Where's the money?"

"It's in a safe and you'll need a passcode for it, and you ain't gettin' it. Simple as that, *baby doll*."

Kara shot the gun to the ceiling. Candace fell to her knees in a quiet whimper. "You'd really rather die tonight than cough up the money? I could shoot you right now and call it self-defense!"

Tom tossed his head back, nodding to the corner of the room. Kara looked up to see a camera. "Three of them in this room. Audio-enabled. Come on. Y'all just get the hell out of here. It's a wash. No one loses."

"Kara. He's right. Let's just go," Candace begged.

Kara planted her feet harder to the ground. She was holding the power of metal and fire in her hands, and yet she felt completely powerless, once again, like the day Child Protection Services had put her back into her mother's arms after she'd run away. She was six years old.

Tom chuckled with a sardonic grin. Candace's eyes pleaded in pity.

Kara heaved deep, her chest springing out. "Let's go. Fuck this shit. Get behind me. We'll keep the gun pointing at him as we walk out. You stay seated motherfucker."

Tom sat with his robe open, a naked body revealed, a belly bulge hanging over his crotch. "Fucking nasty whore."

His words sliced through her like a boxcutter knife. "You're nothing but a nasty pedophile!"

When she and Candace got to the door, they bolted, slamming it behind them, running to remember where the front door was. It felt less like a house now, and more like a rat maze. Candace was still sobbing. They found the front door, flying out of the house like fledgling birds towards Dusty who started the car.

*****

Tuesday Afternoon

Kara

Kara slammed her bedroom door, hard enough to knock the cheap pictures off the hallway's walls. Her mother came behind it, beating the door. "You little bitch! You think you've had it so bad? You have no clue what I went through as a child."

She heard her mother slide down the door, drunkenly tapping it with her knuckles. Kara slumped to the bottom of the door, too. This was her mother's routine. To tell Kara how bad *her* childhood had been, to blame Kara for everything that went wrong after her birth.

"It's not all about what happened to you mom! I was a little girl."

Kara's mother began to whine in long wails. "He used to rape me you know, and my mother knew. She didn't do anything. I've never let anything like that happen to you and what do I get? An ungrateful bitch. A wanna-be cry-baby. That's what you are, Kara."

Kara stood up, kicking the door so hard her foot stung through thick boots. "Go lay down, mom or I'm calling the fucking cops!" She kicked the door again. "Now!"

She listened as her mother stood up, and bumped into walls, finding her way to bed, cursing bitterly. Kara stood like a statue for minutes that slowly turned into an hour, until all sounds were long gone. Not even the flinch of a mouse's eye moving. She opened the door of her room, slowly, to face the darkness of the rest of the house. She walked into her mother's room, where her mom lay sprawled out on a princess bed. Her grandmother had left it for Kara when she had died, but her mother had taken it for herself.

Kara sat at the edge of the bed, as her mother opened her eyes. "Kara, you came here to hold mama?"

Kara crawled onto the bed beside her mother, sitting frog-legged with her mother's head resting in her lap. She moved her eyes over the room. Cluttered with junk, dust, depression, and bitterness with a caustic bite. She began to move her fingers through her mother's hair. Black hair – like her hair – only her mother's was mixed with gray strands. Her mother was born to be a beautiful woman; she had seen the pictures of her mother as a young woman. Now, all she could see was a tired face, wrinkles running down high cheek bones curving along a strong jawline. Her mother's eyes were dark – piercing dark – like her own. She closed them as Kara moved over her face, tracing what may have once been a smile.

"Mother, why did you have me?"

Her mother barely opened her eyes. "What do you mean? I wanted to be loved. What do you mean, Kara?"

"What was the point? I mean you've been a terrible mother," Kara said, reaching her hands around her mother's plump neck, gently at first, but then she squeezed tightly, thinking of Candace breaking up with her after *Mission Easy* had flopped, telling her:

'*Kara, you're just too broken. I can't help you.*'

She thought about the old man mocking her for days afterward via text, calling her a '*dumb whore,*' and her own mother's words, '*you little bitch.*'

Her mother began to fight and squirm, but she was weak from years of pills, and booze. Kara thought about the nights she sat at Starbucks waiting for rides, and how that made her want to rob Tom, so that she could get a car and escape. She thought about the day – a memory that haunted her – the C.P.S worker forcing her out of his arms and back into the arms of her mother after she had run away once. She remembered the woman who had found her on one of these occasions, and given her food. She remembered how soft, kind, and loving the woman had been, and how she thought she had found a new mommy. But then the social workers came, taking her back home. She remembered begging them not to take her back. But they did.

Her mother's hands began to fail, and her eyes began to bulge out of a face turning red. Her mother struggled to breathe.

"Because of you. Because of you," Kara said, continuing to squeeze her mother's neck so tight that her fingers began to cramp.

Her mother flung her arms even more violently, and a wheezing sound trembled from her lips turning blue.

"Did you ever think... Did it ever occur to you that you would have to love me back?"

Eventually the life in her mother's hands went limp, and

Kara felt it, and her ears began to ring as if a plane had crashed in the room, its engine buzzing against her head.

She threw her head back and screamed to drown out the sound, finally letting go of her mother's lifeless neck.

The Disappearance of Professor Peters
Lena Ng

An authoritative knock rattled the door. Under normal circumstances, a person such as you or I, would probably not open the door, especially when alone and at this time of night. But this was not under normal circumstances and, unfortunately, Professor Elizabeth Johnson, a no-nonsense intellectual woman of middle years, had been expecting this late visit. Without hesitation, she arose from her writing desk, strode to the front door, and opened it.

In her presence, two solemn police Inspectors removed their hats. "Professor Johnson?" the older Inspector began. The professor nodded. The older man, likely in his early sixties with a well-worn look on his face, continued. "I'm Inspector Bailey and this," he indicated with a slight movement of his head, "is my partner Inspector Duncan. May we come in?" The Inspector put out his hand. "Thank you for taking time out of your busy schedule to answer our questions."

Prof. Johnson shook the outstretched hand and then the hand of the younger, greener-looking Inspector Duncan, who looked vaguely uncomfortable, or at the very least ill at ease. She would guess the young man had not yet paid enough late-night visits to think of it as just another part of the job. She opened the door wider and both gentlemen stepped inside the small, yet stately, house. After hanging their hats and coats on the conveniently situated oak hallstand, they followed Professor Johnson into what would best be described as a formal sitting room. Here they both seated themselves upon the upholstered couch.

"May I get you gentlemen a cup of coffee?" Except for a slight blanching of the skin, Professor Johnson seemed remarkably composed. It was not every day that a brace of police Inspectors showed up on her doorstep to discuss a missing colleague. But such was the pragmatism of Prof. Johnson's character that, even in the most distressing of situations, the niceties of civility could be maintained.

"It's a little too late for coffee," Inspector Bailey replied. "Water will be fine."

"And for me," Inspector Duncan said.

After returning with three clinking glasses of water, Prof. Johnson seated herself upon the adjacent loveseat.

Inspector Bailey took a sip from the glass before pronouncing, "We have found the body of your colleague, Professor Peters."

"What?" – she recomposed herself – "has happened to him?" Prof. Peters had been missing for three days and now Prof. Johnson's worst fears appeared to be confirmed.

"He had drowned. His wife referred us to you. She didn't know too much about her husband's work." Both Bailey and Duncan drank slowly from their glasses. Inspector Bailey continued. "I know you have many questions, Professor, but maybe we'll be better able to answer them if we learn more about your colleague."

Prof. Johnson nodded. "Of course I'll do anything in my power to help with the investigation."

Inspector Duncan, who, in Prof. Johnson's eyes, looked barely older than any one of her students, pulled out a small notebook from his back pocket. "What does—did— Professor Peters research?"

Prof. Johnson held her glass of water between pale hands. "Professor Peters—Bill—was a parasitologist." Inspector Duncan blinked a couple of times but said nothing. At the younger man's blank expression, she clarified. "He studied parasites."

Inspector Duncan started to look greener than when he first stood in the doorway. "Parasites. You mean, as in leeches? Tapeworms?" At Prof. Johnson's nod, Inspector Duncan pulled back into his chair. "Sounds, uh, fascinating." He made a face that showed what he really meant was 'repellant.'

Prof. Johnson took a small sip from her glass. "It is quite fascinating, actually. At least, Bill found it so."

"Tell us more about his work," Inspector Bailey said.

Prof. Johnson took a deep breath. "The way Bill spoke about his subjects—despite their awful reputation—you could see he was passionate about his work." Upon observing two sceptical looks, Prof. Johnson leaned forward in her chair. "You may think of parasites as disgusting creatures. They feed off a host, such as a leech, as Inspector Duncan mentioned—" she glanced at the young man, "—or a vampire bat. But some of them are more complex. Much more complex. Some have evolved to take over the minds of their hosts and control their behaviour."

"Do you mean like in that movie, Invasion of the Body Snatchers?" Inspector Duncan's raised eyebrows were almost comical in its horror. His expression was also tinged, however, with disbelief.

The corners of Prof. Johnson's mouth pulled upwards in a slight smile. "Yes, to an extent. Take, for example, the parasite *Toxoplasma gondii*. Normally, rats will avoid places that smell of cat urine. But *T. gondii*-infected rats will do the exact opposite—they develop an attraction to the smell and will seek out areas reeking of it. Not only this, but they will confront and harass any cats they find. Of course, cats being cats, they will kill and eat them. The parasite then propagates in the cat, their natural host, before being shed in their waste. Other rats will then eat parasite-contaminated food and the life-cycle of the parasite renews."

Inspector Duncan, scribbling as fast as he could in his small jotter, looked up from his notes. "Was that what the Professor was studying?"

"No, but he was studying another mind-controlling parasite, a hairworm called *Spinochordodes tellinii*." Prof. Johnson tried not to chuckle at Inspector Duncan's deepening look of disgust though she would agree that mind-controlling parasites do sound rather alarming. "Once the larvae, implanted in a grasshopper, has grown, it causes the host to jump into the closest body of water. The grasshopper drowns and the parasite gnaws its way through the grasshopper's head into the water where it reproduces and lays its eggs."

Inspector Bailey tapped the glass between his hands. "You seem so knowledgeable, Professor. Were you involved in his work?"

Prof. Johnson shook her head. "No, but Bill was enthusiastic about his field and spoke of it whenever we ran into each other. I know very little compared to him." She peered over her spectacles. "Instead, I study fungus."

A short-lived look of relief passed over Inspector Duncan. "Fungus. Doesn't sound very appetizing, either. But at least they can't control you."

Prof. Johnson's eyes crinkled at its corners. "Actually, a fungus called *Ophiocordyceps unilateralis* can control its prey. Infected ants turn into zombies, abandoning their nest for the humid forest floor which happens to be the perfect place for fungal growth. The ants use their jaws to latch onto a leaf where they remain until they die. The ripening bodies of the fungus grow large enough to burst from the ant's head, rupturing the fungus so it can release its spores."

Inspector Bailey was seasoned enough to control a shudder but Inspector Duncan wasn't. "Gah," he said. "Imagine what would happen if those parasites could control people."

"They can, in a way," Prof. Johnson replied. "*T. gondii* which controls rats might also be able to control humans. It is a common and wide-spread parasite. It has been researched that owning a cat during childhood increases the risk for developing mental disorders that alter dopamine levels, such as bipolar disorder or schizophrenia. Infection with the parasite has also been associated with less inhibition in risky or frightening situations. For example, carrying the parasite doubles the risk of getting into a car accident. Maybe they can control us in ways we don't yet know about."

Inspector Bailey drew his brows together. "From what you tell us, it sounds like Professor Peters was satisfied with his work. Would there be any reason for him to be depressed?"

"What do you mean?"

"I mean, the manner of his death. Drowning." Inspector Bailey sipped from his glass. "There was no trauma to the body nor any other indication of a struggle. No one heard or saw anything out of the ordinary these past three days he was missing. It would be logical to think he committed suicide."

"No, he wasn't depressed." Prof. Johnson looked puzzled. She tilted her head. "But he did have some medical problems before he disappeared."

"Such as?"

"He was drinking a lot of water which he never did before. It was almost as if he couldn't get enough of it. He thought he was developing diabetes—excessive thirst is one of its symptoms—since it runs in his family. But he also noticed something strange. He saw a small raised mark on his arm. As though something had bitten him. He mentioned he had made an appointment with his family doctor for later this week. He vanished before keeping it."

Inspector Bailey mulled over her words. His water glass was three-quarters empty, yet he still felt thirsty. "Would there be any reason for him to be at the town reservoir?"

"The reservoir? No, none at all. In fact, he hated the water. He almost drowned as a child and had been phobic ever since," Prof. Johnson replied. An odd thought made a brief flash through her mind, but it was too outlandish to stay there.

Inspector Duncan flipped through the pages of his jotter and read over his notes. "Parasites controlling animals, possibly people. Making them do things they never would do.

Studied grasshoppers who drown themselves so parasite can escape into the water system. Professor Peters, possibly bitten, thirsty all the time, hating water but found drowned in the town reservoir. Is all this correct?"

Prof. Johnson slowly nodded. The odd thought returned, sitting on the edge of her mind's horizon. Why would she have the urge to go for a swim? The three of them sat and pondered, and pondered and sat, thinking and thinking as they took sip after another long sip of life-giving water.

Bang on the Money
Ginny Swart

Mandarin Hotel – Tuesday 16th May

"Mister Marrick? Mister Marrick!?"

The 17 year-old hotel foyer busboy at the Mandarin Hotel, Singapore, continued to wander around the reception area, calling for "Mister Marrick!" – a dark brown envelope clutched in his white-gloved hand.

From a black leather armchair towards the rear of the foyer came the call: "Here." Which was followed by a raised hand.

The busboy immediately went over, relieved at finding the man so quickly. "Here, sir, a package for you." Before he was prepared to hand it over, Marrick had to sign the young man's docket as proof of delivery.

From a jacket pocket, Marrick took out a silver penknife and carefully slit open the thick envelope. Inside were two carefully cut sheets of cardboard, taped together, between which was a bronze coloured key. The number 215 was impressed into the top.

Written on one of the cardboard sheets were the words 'Changi – PP2509B – 1530'

Marrick checked his watch – 12:55.

He raised his hand again, calling 'Here,' and the attentive busboy appeared at his side. "I need a taxi in the next five minutes. Tell the doorman it's for Mister Marrick, room 1011."

The boy's enthusiastic "Very good, sir," earned him a $5 tip.

Five minutes later, to the 'tock' Marrick got into the back of the yellow and green taxi. The smell of newly polished leather and canned air freshener was familiar but still irritating on the nose.

"Where to, sir?"

"Changi."

"No luggage, sir?"

"None at all. I'm going to meet someone. Do you have a card so I can get you for the journey back to the Mandarin?"

The taxi driver's smile said: *No waiting in the queue for a pickup this time.* "Here, sir. Ask at the booking desk and they will call for you."

And charge accordingly, no doubt, Marrick thought.

After he'd been dropped off, Marrick went through the terminal entrance, paused to get his bearings, then headed over to the large luggage storage lockers along the corridor wall between the TWA check-in and the executive lounge 'curtained, for your discretion.'

215 was easy to find, and with a medium sized suitcase now in hand, Marrick returned the key to the very pleasant woman manning the Airport Information stand.

From there he headed to the washrooms, found a stall,

closed the door and laid the suitcase on top of the toilet bowl. Two clicks and the case lid was thrown back, revealing a carefully folded white shirt, Collingdale Club tie, black shoes and a sports jacket. After changing, Marrick opened the envelope tucked into the lid pocket, counted the money, put that into his inside jacket pocket, then extracted the dark blue passport and plane ticket (one way, Sydney). From the back pocket of his trousers he pulled another blue passport.

Tossing it into the suitcase, he said: "The king is dead. Long live the king." He clipped shut the case, opened the stall door, and made sure no one was using the facilities. From a trouser pocket he took a traveller bottle of talc, shook a small amount of the white powder onto his palm, then finger brushed it through his hair, changing it from professionally dyed dark brown to a more salt&pepper grey. Over by the mirrors and washbasins, he rinsed his hands clean in the end sink by the paper towel trash can, dried them, then Mr. Mike Carlisle left to board the 15:30 Singapore Airways flight to Sydney.

Back in the washroom, by the towel bin, was the medium sized suitcase – all that remained of the now-late Francis J. Marrick – waiting for someone to steal it.

*****

Lucianna Avenue, Rose Bay, Sydney Friday 19th May

Casually he took a second walk past number 17. First time had been on the far side pavement to check for cars in the driveway, gardeners at work, or any other potential interference. This time he was on the house side, resisting temptation to look directly up the white stone driveway.

That's going to be a bugger if there's anything parked out front leaking oil.

He stopped the other side of the driveway and made a show of checking through his suit pockets. The 'I forgot my keys' was always a good routine, because people didn't think twice when you went back and fished the spare key from its hiding place. Or, in this case, palming the recently cut duplicate from his shirt cuff.

Not that anyone was likely to be watching. 4:30pm was always an ideal time. The kids had been back from school for almost an hour, so nannies were rushed off their feet, commuters still had to start their commutes, and generally everyone would be winding down for the Friday evening.

A double twist of the key threw back both the door lock and deadbolt, and the door swung inwards silently. Pause, listen, then into the coolness of the hall and stairway, closing the door quietly behind him.

Again another pause, silently straining to hear any movement from within while putting on a pair of white cotton gloves and admiring the tasteful designer opulence on display. Not so much as to say gaudy – despite the large 18th Century French gilded mirror on the wall – but enough to say never ever been strapped for cash. Not including the contents, he reckoned the value of the place alone would be around the $500,000 mark. The trouble was all the good stuff was far too big to drop into a pocket.

Thankfully, even with all that money, Mr and Mrs Constantine Tylor, were still too tight to pay for residential staff. Asset rich but cash poor? He doubted it. As he turned he caught his reflection in the mirror and couldn't resist a critical look at himself, smoothing his thick dark hair and awarding himself with a wide, confident smile. The practiced kind that crinkled his face into attractive laugh lines. *Still got it, Mike my lad, those grey hairs just add sex appeal.*

Satisfied that Mrs Tylor wasn't in the house, Mike moved down the hallway and into the central lounge. A Harold Abbot original over the mock fireplace, cocktail cabinet by the wall, hardwood floors and a well-padded three piece suite with one of those geometric diamond designs – cushions to match. In front a wood and ceramic tile coffee table had several Art House magazines tastefully displayed on top.

Through one door off to the right was the study – wall to wall bookshelves, mahogany desk prominent. To the left, sun room-cum-conservatory. The basement was the now obligatory Entertainment room and wet bar.

Constantine, like Onassis, had started out an oil man, but had then diversified into Finance.

The study would have a safe behind a bookcase – no doubt a key and combination affair – for all his bonds, papers and ready cash. Probably a passport or two, for those incognito journeys. The safe was too much time, and no real chance of getting into it without the key.

No, as the song went: *The only way is up, baby…*

Plush carpet on the stairs kept everything silent, and on his way up he admired several photographs of Mrs Patrice Tylor – Pattie Tylor as she was so often referred to in the gossip and social columns. Fashionably slim, athletic in some shots, bobbed blonde hair and hazel brown eyes – she took a very nice photo – as did her jewellery. The sort of pieces that could easily fit into a pocket or two.

On the landing, spare guest bathroom, guest bedrooms 1, 2 and 3, and the Master bedroom suite.

Inside the Master – bed made and tidy by casual morning help – he resisted the temptation to draw the curtains. That was the kind of afternoon anomaly that could possibly attract attention. It was straight to the dressing table where, curiously, Mrs Tylor's jewellery box was open and a four row white diamond bracelet was draped half over the front.

If you can't put your toys away, you really don't deserve them.

He picked up the bracelet and was about to drop it into his jacket pocket when movement in the dressing table mirror caught his attention.

It was Mrs Tylor, standing in front of the now open walk-in wardrobe. She was wearing what looked like a Kym original 'Summer Dress' – watercolour style flowers on light cotton, white leather pumps, and an ever popular digital fitbit thing on her wrist. All that was missing was the large brimmed hat set at a slightly jaunty angle, and a tall glass of Pimm's No. 1. In place of the Pimm's was a decidedly unsociable blue steel 9mm automatic.

Mike slowly raised his hands and carefully turned round to face her. It was obvious from her expression, and the steadiness of her hand, that she knew which end of a gun was which – and more importantly, how to use it.

He turned on his smile. "I can appreciate home defence, but don't you think that's a little excessive? I mean, can we not just talk about this?"

"What's to talk about? You're here attempting to steal my

jewellery. If it wasn't for the fact that blood is difficult to get out of a wool carpet, I suspect I might have shot you before now. Not that the temptation hasn't left me."

"Well, I'll admit that I was attracted by the possibility when I found your front door open. But now I've seen the error of my ways, wouldn't it be for the best to just let me depart? I mean, do I look like a dangerous criminal to you?" He gave her no chance to answer. "No. I'm just a humble common or garden opportunist housebreaker. Harming anyone is beyond me – especially when they're as beautiful as yourself."

"I doubt that very much." She flicked the gun towards the open bedroom door – which gave Mike a clearer view of the weapon, and the fact that the safety catch was still engaged – "I think we should continue this conversation downstairs, Mister…?"

"Tony. Tony Daniels." He extended a hand for shaking, but she just tilted her head slightly.

"Seriously? Look, let's go down to the lounge. It's got to be sunset somewhere in the world, and I know I could do with a gin about now. Also we need to talk."

Well colour me curious. Knowing that the gun was no longer a danger meant he could relax and, hey, why not see what she wanted to talk about? "Okay. Should I lead the way?"

"Well, if you don't, I'll just shoot you in the kneecap. Any preference?"

He shook his head, smiled, then carefully walked down the stairs to the hallway. Pattie Tylor followed at a distance, and Mike found it a little unnerving to notice that the gun didn't waver from the line of his head.

In the lounge she pointed to the sofa. "If you'll kindly sit at the far end while I fix us a couple of tall ones." As he sat, she put the automatic on the coffee table, and their eyes met. She smiled. "If you want to check, the magazine is full of blanks. Oh, and the safety is on."

Over at the cocktail cabinet she set up two highball glasses with a strong Tom Collins mix, brought them over and sat at the other end of the sofa.

Mike tasted his – *heavy on the gin, or what?* – then set it down on the coffee table. "Okay, so what is it you wanted to talk about?"

Pattie took a mouthful of her drink, swallowed, and leaned back against the cushions. "Would you say, in your less than honest opinion, that you were a professional thief, rather than some lucky amateur?"

The question caught him by surprise. "Well, I… Er…" *What a way to start a conversation! He was good. More than good.* "Yes, I'd say I was very professional."

"Except when you get caught, like now."

Was it just an impression, or did Pattie Tylor remind him of a King cobra, trying to decide where to strike first?

She didn't let him answer, but carried on. "You see, Tony – if I may call you that?"

He nodded, then felt a touch embarrassed for not spotting her hint of sarcasm.

"Okay, Tony it is then. But you see, Tony, in my husband's line of work I've probably been introduced to dozens, possibly hundreds of very crooked businessman over the years."

"You must have been a child bride." *Any port in a storm….*

"Well, isn't that sweet – cloyingly so – so do be quiet until I've finished. These men believe themselves to be all powerful. They take what they want, and don't care who gets hurt in the process. I've decided I no longer want to be hurt anymore."

He nearly reached over to comfort her, but then thought better of it.

Instead he leaned back and took a longer sip of his drink. The Bombay Sapphire felt pretty warm on the way down. "So," he coughed into his fist. "Why don't you get a divorce?"

"Divorce? With all the lawyers Constantine has under his thumb? At best I would get less than half of what he'll say he's worth. He wouldn't be Constantine if he hadn't already squirrelled away assets and properties via a shell company or two. We might not have slept together for years, but I do know him very intimately when it comes down to money."

"So…?" Mike let it trail off in order to see how she'd react.

"So, I'd like you to kill him for me. That way everything comes to me, the poor grieving widow, regardless."

Mike's confusion was obvious. "Say what now!?"

"Kill him." She adopted a tone of voice she probably used when talking to very young children. "You know, make him deaded for me."

"Are you serious?" For some reason he felt as if reality had just had an earthquake.

"Of course I'm serious. Why else do you think I'm asking you to do it?"

He finished off his drink in a couple of gulps.

Pattie smiled at him. "Look, I'm going to make it easy for

you." She picked up the 9mm automatic from off the coffee table. "This is Constantine's Browning. It's registered to him, and he's flashed it around amongst friends – even at a dinner party, which was embarrassing in the extreme. So everyone knows he has it." She deftly ejected the magazine. "What everyone doesn't know is that it's only ever been loaded with blanks."

She showed Mike the top, giving him a clear view of the crimped ends – no metal projectiles.

"But why?"

"Because if someone gets to it before he does he's worried they'll shoot him with his own gun. Isn't that deliciously ironic? Being shot with your own gun. And now you have the chance to make that irony come true."

"What? There's no way–"

"Fifty thousand – pounds, not dollars." She stood up and went over to the cocktail cabinet. From behind the chrome shaker she pulled out a plain manila envelope and tossed it over to him. "You can count it if you feel you must. What do they say?" She looked thoughtful. "No honour amongst thieves?"

Mike didn't open the envelope – it felt satisfyingly weighty – but put it in his inside jacket pocket. He put an arm across the back of the sofa. Fifty large was not to be sniffed at. "So, you want me to shoot him with his own gun?"

"Most certainly." She walked back to him with the magazine carefully held between finger and thumb. "However, I've some 9mm bullets in my wardrobe. A couple of months ago Constantine and his obsequious little sidekick, Paulo

Stichi, took me down to some Country Club shooting range. Apparently it was supposed to be exciting and fun." She made a little scrunch of her lips. "They gave me a box of 50 rounds and basically left me to my own devices, so I divided the ammunition up equally between a Glock 17 and the pockets of my gilet."

She turned and headed for the door into the hall. "I'll go up and load this for you. Make yourself comfortable. Get yourself another drink, or you can pocket the cigarette lighter, you know, to keep your hand in. It's a good one – solid silver and made by Dunhill." Then she headed on up to the master bedroom.

Mike sat back and blew out a long sigh. The money – *oh, boy, the money!* – was very, very tempting. He'd have to adjust his plans, do some surveillance perhaps? Maybe Pattie would give him her husband's itinerary? His thoughts were interrupted by Pattie's return.

"There you are, all nice and deadly." She showed him the top round in the magazine – clean brass, and a small length of steel at the end. She picked up the Browning, then put it back down again.

"You know what?"

Mike was too stunned to reply, so she carried on.

"I think I'll keep this one," she slid the top round out of the magazine and looked at it for a couple of seconds before she popped it in her dress pocket. "It'll make a lovely keepsake." Then she pushed the magazine back into the grip of the automatic.

Still aghast at her coldness, he said, "You're really serious about this."

"Of course I am. So, when can you do it? Tomorrow's Saturday, and Monday he's off to Malta, I think. How about Sunday, after church? Constantine is Greek Orthodox, but don't let that hold you back."

Mike shook his head. Things were getting out of his control. He'd come here to do a job, but it certainly wasn't this one.

"Look, something like this will take weeks – maybe months of planning."

Pattie put her hand in her pocket and pulled out a small square of paper. "Here's the address of his… Well, I suppose she's his mistress. He sees her every Thursday night." Again the thoughtful pause, then, "An extra twenty-five thousand if you shoot the pair of them when they're in bed together. The papers would love that. Maybe I could sell an exclusive as the first cuckold of spring?"

That had been it for Mike. He stood up from the sofa and snatched the automatic off the coffee table. Pattie stood up, surprise registering on her face. "What's going on?"

"I'm sorry, Mrs Tylor, but your husband has already given me a payment to kill you. And as you know, Constantine is not a man you cross."

Then he shot her three times in the chest, almost point blank range.

As she dropped to the floor he looked over at her. It was sort of hard to tell where the bullets had entered her body because the watercolour flower design was mostly of bright red poppies.

Miraculously she started to move, putting her hand on the coffee table to help herself up, and Mike immediately pointed the gun at her.

Opening her eyes, she said, "Don't do that again."

In seconds she was back up on her feet. "I never realised how much that wadding would hurt. I know they use blanks in the theatre, but even so."

Mike looked at the Browning in his hand, then back at Pattie. "Blanks?" His confusion was back, big time.

She brushed at the front of her dress where the 3 sooty powder burns were. "Looks like I'm going to have to say goodbye to this nice thing as well, as I can't see the dry cleaners being able to remove much of this. Nice grouping though. You really are a professional at this aren't you."

Mike sat down on the sofa again. "You switched live ammunition for blanks?"

Pattie reached behind the nearest throw cushion and came back up with a simple chrome revolver.

"There, that's better." She remained standing. "The whole thing is loaded with blanks, except for the one I took off the top. Oh," she pointed the revolver at his feet. "That little Walther you have in the ankle holster – the one you were supposed to shoot me with – you can put it on the table now."

"How did you–"

"Well, Mike – can I call you Mike now? When you're married to an over-confident im-potentate, sometimes you become invisible. Constantine left the receipt for that little pistol under a stack of papers on his desk. That, and the fact I've had one of our bank staff provide me with monthly statements of his accounts – on pain of ritual castration, naturally. That's where I saw the money go out." She transferred the revolver to her left hand and her right danced over the touchscreen of the fitbit. "And now, of course, I have your incriminating confession recorded and uploaded to the Internet somewhere." The revolver returned to her right hand. "Isn't technology a wonderful thing?"

Mike leaned forwards as he hitched up his trouser leg – hearing the loud click as Pattie thumbed back the hammer of the revolver. "Be careful how you take it out. Now put it on the floor and kick it over here." She put her shoe on it, then nudged it under the sofa, safely out of reach.

He looked at her. "So all that about killing your husband was a charade?"

"Good heavens yes. Why should I want him dead? He's got far too much earning potential left in him, and with your confession I have the perfect leverage."

"Blackmail?"

"Why Mister Carlisle, blackmail is such an ugly word. I much prefer demanding money with menaces. This recording will keep me in a nice monthly income for at least several decades – maybe more if I can get him to shed some weight and eat more healthily."

"And the money?" Mike's hand moved towards his inside jacket pocket – but Pattie flicked the muzzle of the revolver at him.

"Easy, tiger. No, you can keep the money. There's three thousand, in used notes, and the rest is all movie money – Hollywood jiggery fakery. There should be enough for you to pick up an airline ticket to Europe – though I'd make it several hops to help cover your tracks. As you say, my husband isn't someone you would want to cross, even accidentally. If you hurry, you should be able to make one of the late evening flights."

Mike stood and she followed him down the hall to the front door. Opening it, he walked out of the house, then turned as if to say something.

Looking at her now, he realised that not only was she was a very beautiful woman, but also intelligent, and as hard as a diamond.

He opened his mouth, but she just closed the door in his face. No wonder Constantine had wanted to see the last of her.

Christine de Pizan and the Chest Full of Furs

Sandrine Bergès

Paris – 1397

The day was not going well.

Dame Eliza was sitting across from Christine and was explaining in her thick Nordic accent that she would not be buying the collection of poems after all. She was making the point again, after describing in details how she had discovered her husband in the pantry with the scullery maid and decided that a book of love poetry would not, after all, make a suitable anniversary present.

The book was more than halfway done. Christine had spent days copying her poems, neglecting her new work, because she needed the money more than the intellectual stimulation. Of course, she could always change the first page and sell the book to another customer, but it was frustrating nonetheless. And she could just imagine what her mother would say:

Customers are unreliable, you can't expect to earn enough to keep your children fed with writing.

That would then be followed by the inevitable suggestion that she meet this or that nice gentleman, who also happens to be looking for a new wife.

Christine took a deep breath and opened a book - she was reading Nicole d'Oresme's book of geometry. Oresme had been a friend of her father, and a great source of texts for those, like her, who didn't know Greek. And since she made such use of his translations of Plato and Aristotle, she felt she owed it to him to read his own work. But this was not a compliment she looked forward to paying as she had heard her father referring to it as one of the most arduous works he'd ever read. Also, her Latin was a bit rusty.

She was, however, saved from reading past the first line by her mother bursting into her room in a flurry of excitement and indignation.

"Christine! Whatever are you thinking of?! A large chest being delivered here, at this time of day! With the servants all but one out on errands and no-one to carry it up to your rooms!"

Christine put her book down. This was unusual: she had not been expecting a delivery, and if she had, it would have been only paper and ink. Heavy, perhaps, but not like a chest.

"Let's go down and have a look then, mother."

The chest was large. And heavy. The men who had delivered it had left it in front of the house, and refused to take it inside.

Christine considered for an instant opening it on the street, bringing its contents inside, and then carrying the empty box. She changed her mind when she spied a young girl lurking nearby, about 12 years old, dressed in reasonably clean rags. Christine snapped her fingers and the girl came closer.

"Sarah, are your brothers working today?"

"No, Dame Christine. They're at the tavern."

"Can you fetch them for me and say that if they're sober enough to carry this chest inside, there'll be half a day's wage for them."

"Yes, Dame Christine." Sarah approximated a curtsey and ran off to the end the street.

"I don't know how you can possibly have any relationship with such people," her mother scolded. "I don't want these men in my house. They will steal or break things."

"Jean and Marc are fine, mother. They're lazy, but when they do work, they work well." She didn't add *Besides it's not your house, mother*, but her mother's frown told her that she'd heard it nonetheless. Christine felt a pang. There'd been a time when her relationship with her mother was not strained - the ten years she'd had a husband. Her mother had been great helping raising the children, when her beloved was at war, and she'd been great for the first few months of her widowhood, running the household while Christine cried and wrote love poetry. But then the question came between them: *when will you marry again?* For Christine the answer was *never*. She'd been lucky once, but she knew too much about the world to hope for luck a second time. She enjoyed her independence too, and now that she'd succeeded in getting hold of her widow's pension, her books were enough to keep the family fed and warm.

Dame Florence stood with her daughter on the street, hugging her narrow rib-cage against the early spring cold. At last the men arrived. Neither seemed particularly inebriated and both had an open and pleasant countenance. They asked Christine where they needed to take the box and within minutes, it was standing in one of the upstairs rooms. Christine thanked them and told them to see her agent later in the day when he was back from visiting their lawyers. Then the two women were alone with the chest.

"Shall we?" asked Christine. Her mother nodded.

First there was a great deal of dust. Then, a layer of oiled cloth, which looked questionable, but which Christine removed, carefully putting it down in the lid of the box, so that it did not dirty the carpet on the floor (a legacy from her father who had bought it in Venice). And then, a fur.

Christine took a step back, expecting moths, or other fur loving pests to come rushing out. But none did, so she approached again, and put her hand on its softness. It was black, and quite shiny. She took it out. A large cloak. One that would do for a man as well as a woman. And in perfect condition. She dug further in the chest: some accessories, made out of the same animal. Russian sable? Mink? And then another large item, and another, and yet one more. And for each of them, hats, hand warmers, neck scarves. Now her mother was at the chest with her, running her hands through the beautiful furs, white and brown, as well as black.

"Who sent you this? Did you pay for it?"

"Of course not! I have no idea where it came from. Let's look and see if there is a letter."

But the chest, once empty, revealed no word of its provenance. Christine and her mother took turn to speculate on the carvings and paintings.

"It's a wedding chest," said Dame Florence.

"What makes it different from any other chest, mother?"

asked Christine.

"There's a pair of doves engraved at the front. That means union."

"But it could mean peaceful union, it could be a present that goes with a peace treatise between two families"

Her mother snorted, "Not much of that going on at the moment, I'm afraid."

Christine nodded: her mother was right. Families that were warring were not making up, and had not for at least half a century.

"Let's say it is a wedding chest," she conceded. "Why would there be only furs in it? What about linen and wool? And more to the point," she added, "Why would anyone send us their wedding chest?"

"Well," replied Dame Florence, reluctantly letting go of a fine handwarmer, "I guess we should keep them safe until we find out who they do belong to."

*****

The following day was a regular day. Christine received a new commission for a book of love poems, and she got working on finishing the one she had started. Because it was for an older couple, she decided to add a poem about longevity, and cherishing each other for a life time. Not that Christine had experienced that, being widowed in her twenties, but she could imagine what such life might have been.

Towards the end of the afternoon, a note was delivered. Nothing mysterious this time and only pleasurable. Her friend, Dame Agnes, was feeling better, and asked for her to come over the next day for a visit. Christine replied immediately that she would love too, and then went down to help her mother supervise the end of the children's school day. They had been playing between lunchtime and mid afternoon, and then were back at their Latin until dinner time. Florence did not know Latin, and did not think much of little girls learning it. But since her grandson at least had to know it, she made sure to watch over them as well as she could. Christine, who'd been taught it by her father, and was able to do a little more, set them versions and supervised repetition of declensions and conjugations. They would be better off with a tutor, but for that, she'd need to earn more. Then dinner came and the evening passed without any of them thinking about the chest full of furs.

The next morning as Christine was preparing to set off to visit her friends her mother stopped her:

"Are you going to Agnes dear? May I join you? I was meaning to talk to her cook about the herbs she's had brought back from their country house and take some cuttings."

Christine nodded. She had been looking for a bit of privacy with her friend, but she suspected her mother would spend much of her time in the herb garden with the cook. Dame Florence was a keen gardener and knew her way around plants. And although she'd denied vehemently that it had anything to do with scientific knowledge, she was in fact quite experimental with her cuttings, and could use herbs for both medicinal and culinary purposes.

They did not take the carriage, as the weather was pleasant, and the walk no longer than half an hour, so why spend money that could so easily be saved? Agnes was better indeed, and she was down in the small reception room that she kept for private visitors, rather than in her bed, where Christine had visited her most often. She was pale still, and her chair had been brought closer to the fire than would feel comfortable for a healthy person. Christine wondered, as she did every time she saw her friend, how many more visits they would have together.

Agnes, it turned out, was not alone. Behind her stood a small adolescent girl, trying hard to disappear behind the drapes of the chair.

Agnes drew her out gently, and introduced her to Christine and Dame Florence: "This is Olivia, whose mother was a close friend of mine. She is staying with me until she is married in a few months' time"

Christine nodded. It was not unusual for brides to be to sent out of their homes in the months preceding their marriage, to get them out of the way of preparations, and get them used to living away from home. Olivia looked like she was barely fifteen, and still a child. But Christine caught something in her eye as she offered her greetings that made her think she may in fact be quite grown up in some ways.

"Who are you marrying, child?" asked Florence.

"A gentleman from Venice," Agnes replied on her behalf. "Olivia is to move there after they are married."

"Well this is where we are from, my husband and I," replied Florence. "It may be that we know his family?"

"His name is Blasio di Parma, my Lady," supplied Olivia. "His family is recently settled in Venice and his father distinguished himself in the battle against the Genoese."

"Yes," said Dame Florence, vaguely. "I think I know of the name."

"Do you know your husband to be, Olivia?" asked Christine. It was not customary for a bride to be introduced to her groom before the wedding.

"I have seen a portrait," replied Olivia, bringing a heavy medallion that was hanging around her fragile neck from her dress. Christine and her mother gathered around it. It was a miniature portrait of a young man, who may have been either attractive or unprepossessing, but did not, in any case, have any obvious repulsive traits. Or at least, none that the painter had felt compelled to reproduce for his bride to be.

"Sir Blasio is a handsome man," said Christine. "I hope you and he will be very happy together."

"Thank you my Lady," Olivia nodded.

Then it was time for the refreshments. Agnes asked Olivia to go to the kitchen to ask after them, and Dame Florence decided to follow her and see to her own business with the cook. So it was that Christine and her friend were left alone.

"She is young to be married," started Christine.

"She is the age you were, or thereabouts," replied Agnes.

"I was lucky, but many aren't." And then to change the subject, as she suspected her unmarried friend would go on to argue that any marriage, no matter how bad, was better than none: "How did she come to be sent to you?"

"I'm not entirely sure, to tell the truth. I knew her mother a little, and I know her grandmother and my mother were close, but both are long dead, and it was her governess who wrote to me and asked if she could stay. Her father knew, of course. The idea came from him, I think."

"I guess they must have wanted her out of the way while her

things were packed to go to Venice."

Agnes nodded, "Very likely, and what better distraction than coming to Paris?"

The friends paused to consider that Agnes's home was hardly the life and soul of the capital. She was almost always sickly, and received very few visitors when she wasn't. But maybe part of the deal was that Olivia would be company for Agnes, and that, thought Christine, was a good thing.

After Florence had finished her business with the cook, she and Christine said their goodbyes to Agnes, and Christine promised to come back the next day with a carriage to take Olivia out.

As soon as they were home and had taken off their coats, Florence rushed off and came back, grabbed her daughter's hand and took her to the room where they had left the chest. 'I knew it!' she exclaimed.

"Knew what?" asked Christine, somewhat impatiently.

Florence pointed to a pattern on the wooden lid. Above the doves, a small bouquet of violets surrounded by ferns. "This," she said. "I saw the same pattern on a casket in the kitchen at Agnes's."

"Why would she keep a casket in the kitchen?" asked Christine.

"She doesn't! It was full of herbs and tinctures that young women take when they are to be married. Things to ease the onset of pregnancy".

"So it was Olivia's? Well, that's very interesting, mother. What do you make of it?"

"I make nothing of it except that she must have sent her

things to the wrong address, somehow, and we should return it as soon as possible. But it will cost to have it carried there."

"But Agnes didn't mention lost luggage," And if she is going to Venice, why would she need all these furs?"

"How should I know? Ask her, not me!"

"That's exactly what I shall do," replied Christine.

*****

Christine waited, the next day, until she and Olivia were safely in the carriage. She had offered to take her to court, not to meet the queen, but to ride through the gardens. But once they were alone, she did not hold back:

"I have your box," she said. "You have beautiful furs. Do you want to tell me why it's in my house?"

Olivia, looked away. But when she turned back there were tears in her eyes. "I didn't know what else to do."

"Why don't you tell me what happened?" asked Christine, more kindly, after she offered her a lemon scented handkerchief.

Olivia blew her nose loudly, showing that she still was, in some ways, a child.

"I didn't want to go to Venice," she said. "I was going to Denmark. I was to be married to my best friend, from childhood, and he was to take up a post there. But then my father decided I should make for a more advantageous match, and he found this merchant from Italy, whom I'd never met. And he told Johan to go away and never come back." She took a breath "So we decided that I would go with him anyway. That we would be married here, in Paris, and that we would travel together to Denmark. But I had to keep it a secret from my parents. I couldn't take my winter clothes with me - they wouldn't have been needed in Venice."

Christine nodded. "But why send them to me?"

"My mother had a few letters from Dame Agnes's from a long time ago, and the last one had your address on it, and it said she was visiting you. I thought that maybe you were still in touch, and that if not, it wouldn't be so hard to find your house and get my chest back."

Christine thought about the way her mother had eyed up the furs when they first opened the box. "You were taking a risk. What would stop me if I just wanted to keep them for myself?"

"I know," replied Olivia, "But I thought, from the letter, that you were a good person, and I just didn't know what else to do with them."

"So what now?" asked Christine after a pause.

"Now, nothing!" Olivia started to cry again. "I haven't heard from Johan since I arrived. He was supposed to get in touch, but he's not replied to my note and I don't know what else to do!"

Christine managed to comfort the girl by promising she'd try and find out what had happened to her sweetheart, and the rest of the day went by peaceably. When she dropped her off, Christine asked Olivia to tell Agnes everything she had told her. She said that she would visit the next day and that together they would think the matter through.

And when Christine got home she found that she had to involve one more person. Her mother was waiting for her, impatient to hear what had happened after she confronted

Agnes. Christine considered briefly fobbing her off with a tale of a wrong address. But then decided that there was no point as her mother would soon ferret out the truth, and that perhaps that ferreting out would be best put to use solving the mystery of Johann's disappearance.

Her mother was immediately interested. "We must find out who that young man was supposed to work with in Denmark. Surely he must have a contact here in Paris. Or somebody who was in Paris recently and went back to Denmark. Who do we know who is connected to that country?"

It came to Christine almost immediately: "Dame Eliza! The one who had commissioned that book of poetry and who cancelled it a few days ago."

"Why did she cancel again?"

"Because she caught her husband having congress with one of the housemaid, and decided he didn't deserve a gift of love poems."

"Quite right too," replied Florence. "But what do they have to do with Denmark?"

"Eliza is part of Queen Margrethe's entourage!" replied Christine, excitedly. "Her husband is a court doctor, I think, and he may well have hired an apprentice."

"Well, is this Johann an apprentice doctor?

"I don't know," replied Christine. "I didn't think to ask."

*****

The very next day they found out. Johann was a trained apothecary, and had decided to try and learn medicine too, which is why he had been employed by Eliza's unfaithful husband. The mystery of his early departure was solved too.

After the disgrace of being found out, Sir Gregoire had thought it expedient to leave immediately, and he had taken his apprentice with him.

If the journey had been swift, and the horses changed without delay, there would have been no chance of stopping long enough to write a letter, which would explain Johann's silence. The question remained: what should be done next. Agnes was very unhappy about letting her friend's daughter enter a marriage against her will, and against her heart. Despite the usual reassurance that husbands and wives would grow to love each other, this was much harder if one loved elsewhere. They had established that no child would be born from Olivia that might compromise her union with the Venetian. But transferring love from one man to another was still a tricky matter. Or even tolerating one man's presence in one's bed, if one was hoping to be with another.

But Agnes also did not want to go against the girl's family - that is, she did not want to enable her to rebel against her father's authority. This could have dire consequences for Olivia, as well as for Johan.

The solution came to them within three days via two very sad pieces of news.

First, Olivia finally heard from Johan. He apologized, sheepishly, for disappearing when they were on the brink of eloping. But he also said he realized that it would take him months, maybe years, before he could make a place for her by his side, and that maybe Denmark was not the best place for them to settle. He advised Olivia to marry the Venetian and forget all about him. And then, a letter came from Venice, to say that the Venetian had succumbed to disease and thus all her wedding plans were cancelled at once. Olivia was upset, of course. She mourned her lost love, and even the loss of the man she was to marry - she hadn't, even in her worst moods, wished him dead.

She was also in no hurry to go home, and her father did not claim her. Agnes, although she enjoyed her company, knew that soon she would be too ill again to care for Olivia. Olivia came up with the solution herself. She had no wish to be married off to anyone, and she wanted to go to a convent. Agnes had heard of a place that took young women and educated them, and enabled them to learn a useful trade. And so it was agreed that Christine would accompany her.

The day before the departure, Christine remembered the furs.

"You and Dame Florence should keep them," Olivia said. "I have plenty enough clothing with me, and my dowry can be transferred to the convent."

Christine thanked her on behalf of her mother, and smiled to think that keeping her warm would not require extra work, or money, on her part.

*****

The journey took several days, and was uncomfortable, but when they arrived, Christine was satisfied that Olivia had made the right choice. The Abbess herself received them and they were fed a very pleasant meal - there was no sense that the nuns were made to abstain beyond reason and all seemed very healthy and cheerful. The Abbess then introduced them to the nuns in charge of education. There was a teacher of Greek and Hebrew, and one who taught the use of medicinal herbs. There were painters and even a sculptor, and many women who worked on copying and illuminating books, and Christine immediately saw an opportunity. Should her orders increase, she could ask the nuns here to work for her. And the Abbess also saw something in Christine:

"We are always searching for new knowledge," she told her. "And I hear that you are great source of knowledge, not only in poetry, but also history and other useful sciences."

Christine wondered where the Abbess would have heard all this, and then she noticed a portrait of the Duke of Orleans on the wall behind her table. This was her source, clearly. The Abbess nodded: "Yes, our good Duke even told me that you are researching the art of chivalry?"

"Indeed. Although these are early days yet, and it is not easy for a woman to access the kind of practical knowledge such expertise would require."

"I have an armoury here," said the Abbess. "It was left to me by my late father. I have nuns who require physical exercise, and many private fields where they can take it without anyone noticing." She paused. "If you could see your way to spending a few weeks or months with us, each year, you could practice the art of chivalry with them, and further your knowledge."

Christine's heart leapt at this opportunity. "I would have to speak to my mother and my children of course."

"They are all welcome here. We have space, and we do not lack for food or linen. Come, all of you, and we shall make good use of each other."

Christine thanked her, and went home determined to take

her up on the offer. She sensed that her life was about to take an interesting turn.

They Do Things Better in Albuquerque
Michelle Ann King

They say we forgive someone because we need it, not because they do. I think that's true. I also think we tell someone our secrets not because they need to know but because we want them to.

I tell Den my secrets because I want him to know what he got himself into by marrying me. That's only fair, right?

I'm thirty years old today. When I was a kid I always thought I'd be living in America by now. If we lived in America we could be sitting in a cabin or a lake house. A mountain hideaway in Michigan or a waterfront ranch in Oregon. Somewhere with wooden walls and wild views and beautiful isolation. No neighbours, no traffic noise, nothing but empty sky and the calling of birds. In my mind's eye I see ravens; huge and sleek, black harbingers of doom.

Is that really ravens, or am I maligning them unfairly? I don't know. But if they're not precursors of disaster in real life, they are in my head. And that's where the important stuff happens, after all.

But I don't mind, really, that we stayed here. London, grey

and neon, both frighteningly alive and as full of rotting corpses as any zombie film. We still have an affectionate relationship. Probably because we're so alike.

But if Den and I can't be in the mountains, at least we have snow today. Snow provides the kind of isolation you normally can't get in a city. Blank, buffering snow, masking and silencing the world underneath.

'Have we got a shovel anywhere, Jan?' Den asks. 'In the shed, maybe? I'm sure I've seen one somewhere. I should go out and clear the drive.'

'No,' I say. 'Leave it as is.'

He shrugs. 'All right. Do you want some breakfast?'

'Yes,' I say, although I don't. Den can't cook, but that's a good thing. I have nightmares, and sometimes only the smell of burning bacon can waft them away. The smell of the preparation of dead flesh. It feels like a ceremonial action, the start of a complex ritual that will bring about the end of the world. I think that I have been enacting this ritual for most of my life. I think the ritual is my life.

You can eat nightmares, but most people don't know that. Den doesn't. He doesn't know I eat his. They fill me up.

He left his wife and kids for me, five years ago. He dreams about them a lot, dreams about witches and demons pulling them into bite-sized pieces. In the morning he blames it on too many late nights in front of the Horror Channel.

He shouldn't have left them. I don't think he knows that either, though.

He kept a photo of Baby Harriet in his wallet for a long time. Baby Harriet grew up to be a monstrous teenager, all bile and cheap piercings that she doesn't know how to properly flaunt. I ate her picture, and I know her intimately.

Her mother, Carly, is simply concrete now. No juice left. I'm sorry about that.

No, I'm not.

The snow is still falling, the air thick with glittering white. Would it choke me I went outside and tried to breathe? Maybe. Maybe I'll open the door and find out.

In America, I would be able to breathe easier. Montana, Texas, Alaska; all those wide open spaces providing great lungfuls of air. In America, I wouldn't be the way I am. I wouldn't be who I am. I would keep my accent because you always have to remember where you came from, but I could call myself Bobbie-Sue and say things like *buck naked* and *gotten* and *son of a bitch*.

In South Carolina, I would have humidity and heat rash and go looking for alligators. We're all in a fishbowl, and sometimes they forget to feed us. The water gets murky and I bump my nose against the glass. It's all just lip-synching anyhow.

I have a headache. They usually follow the nightmares. The bacon doesn't help with those much.

Den works in insurance. Received wisdom says that's boring, but I don't think it is. Den doesn't ever seem bored. That's his superpower, I think. You don't want to know what mine is.

'There's something I have to tell you,' I say as Den comes back into the living room with two plates stacked high with bacon sandwiches. In New York, the sandwiches would have fifteen other exotic ingredients and be made with three slices of dark German rye bread. These just have ketchup.

We always eat in the living room, on the sofa, in front of the TV. Even when it's not on. We don't actually watch a lot of TV. My mother used to say that you should always eat at a dining table, otherwise it showed a lack of class. That made me laugh. Still does. But credit where it's due. She was the classiest prostitute I ever met. And I met a lot.

Den puts the plates on the coffee table. I pat the cushion beside me and he sits down. He folds his hands in his lap and looks grave. Den is good at looking grave. I think it comes from all those insurance claims. All those litanies of disaster. Storm, flood, lightning, malicious damage, subterranean fire. I don't even know what that is, but it sounds terrifying. Like the wrath of gods.

He always listens to my secrets but I don't think he always believes them. Does the failing lie with him, or me? Or with the universe? Perhaps there is insufficient verisimilitude in the truth.

'I killed a man once,' I tell him. 'I wanted to kill my father because that's more mythological and myths are how we make sense of the world. But I never knew who he was, and hunting down all my mother's clients from 1973 seemed a little over the top, even for an obsessive like me.'

I wrap my right hand around the left side of my neck. It's a restrictive position, and therefore comforting. It does me good to be restricted. It ought to happen more often.

'So I chose a stand in,' I continue. 'A representation. I don't know if he deserved it, if he was a bad father, a bad man.

Probably. We all are, to some extent. The hero of one story is the villain of another. Myths again, you see? That's how it works.'

If we'd moved to Maine, some small town from a Stephen King novel, I wouldn't have had to do all that by myself. I wouldn't have had to get my hands wet. There would have been a vengeful spirit or a physical manifestation of my psyche to do it for me. But we stayed in Camden, and they don't believe in the supernatural here.

Den puts his hand on my thigh and squeezes. I've heard that squeeze before. It says you're safe, it's okay, I love you.

'I promised him sex, drugged him, laid him out in the bath and razored his wrists. Lengthwise, not crossways. That's how you tell if someone's serious.'

My own scars run in horizontal bands, like bracelets. I never wear long sleeves, even when it's cold. If we lived in Florida, I would never need to. Except that there are no real people in Florida. It's all make believe there. All smoke and mirrors.

'I wrote his suicide note in Esperanto, to add a touch of flair to the proceedings,' I say. I can speak six languages fluently and write decently enough in another four. Plus Klingon, just for the hell of it. Because today is always a good day to die.

Den nods, picks up his bacon sandwich and takes a big bite. I hold mine, inhale the chargrilled smell and put it down again. I don't have much of appetite for food.

I have got—*gotten*, whispers my alter-ego Bobbie-Sue— drunk on absinthe, bitten off a girl's finger during a fight in the school playground when I was six years old, slept with a priest, driven the wrong way around the M25 at 3am. I have killed, I have lied, I have broken faith. I am not human. I am not always real. I have seen attack ships on fire off the shoulder of Orion. No, wait. That last one was science fiction.

I am not who I say I am.

I tell Den these things, but he stays with me, I don't know why. And I have stayed with him, I don't know why. Ennui. Disaffection. Habit. Maybe that's actually the definition of love.

Outside, the snow is still falling.

If we lived in Albuquerque then things would be different. If we lived in Albuquerque then we would… actually, I don't know what we would do. I don't know anything about Albuquerque other than that it has a great name. But I'm sure they do things better there.

'I want to move,' I tell Den. 'Emigrate. To America. To Albuquerque.'

He finishes his sandwich, wipes his mouth and takes a bite out of mine. 'Why?' he says.

Because I think if we live in Albuquerque, I won't kill him.

'I don't know,' I say. 'I just heard it was nice there.'

Seeing the Light
Amanda Steel

"What happened to you?" Owen, her lodger asked, when Carla came downstairs to get breakfast, trying to keep up the pretence she hadn't woken up outside again.

"I slept badly," she replied.

Owen looked doubtful. "That doesn't explain all the scratches."

She'd already caught sight of herself in the hallway mirror. Not even three layers of concealer and foundation had been able to cover up her injuries this time. Her arms were also bruised. Maybe she'd hit them on the trees in her haste to get home before anyone saw her.

"I don't remember." It wasn't hard for her to act baffled about her injuries.

Supressed memories surfaced – Bright lights moving towards her – mechanical sounds – then waking up naked – laying on cold gravel. 4am in the suburbs meant she had been able to make the half mile back to her condo unnoticed. Again.

She could feel Owen watching her back as she poured coffee into a mug. Bowl, cereal, milk. Then she had no choice but to turn round and meet his stare.

"I told you, I just don't remember."

Owen shrugged, took a leaflet out of his back pocket and placed in in front of Carla, next to her coffee.

Mouth half full of cornflakes, she said, "What's that for?"

"I forgot to give you it yesterday. In case you can think of someone who needs it?" Owen gave her a weak smile.

Self-Harming? Help is at Hand. "I don't know anyone who is…oh…I'm not…this was an accident." She raised one of her bruised arms to her face.

Owen's reply of, "Whatever you say," sounded far too sarcastic. He pointed to the empty bottle of Merlot on the countertop. "Maybe that was to blame?" Then he left to catch his morning bus.

She looked at the bottle. *One glass a night shouldn't have this effect on me.*

*****

When Carla arrived at Clancy Street, the road was shut off. Black and white Police cars were parked across the middle of the street, with *Crime Scene – Do Not Cross* tape stretched from sidewalk to sidewalk.

"What the…?" She parked her blue rust bucket of a Ford Nova a block away, walked back to Clancy, then tried to duck under the tape. She managed four steps before an overzealous uniformed cop tried to pull her back by her arm.

She winced as his fingers dug into her bruises. "Hey! I work down here! Petrochelli's Diner. I'm the short order cook!"

Her sweatshirt sleeve rode up, exposing the old and new bruises, making the cop let go. Raising both his hands, he proclaimed, "There's no way I just did that!"

Carla considered saying he did unless he allowed her to get to work, but she couldn't bring herself to resort to emotional blackmail.

"Please, I need to get to work." She heard the whine in her voice. "I can't afford to lose any wages or tips this month."

The cop pointed beyond the cars and their strobing red and blue roof bars. "Look, everything down there is shut for the rest of the day at least, so there's no point in me letting you pass, and you would be disturbing a crime scene."

"What crime scene?"

The cop lowered his voice. "The woman who manages the diner was found next to the fryer, dead. I can't tell you what happened, because even I don't know the details. But believe me, there is no way I can let you past."

Carla stared at him, her mouth hanging open as the colour drained from her face.

"Did you know her?" The cop stood back so he could get a good shot of her on his bodycam.

"She was my boss," Carla managed to say. Her throat felt like it was cutting off her oxygen supply.

"Then we're going to need to talk to you later."

He took her contact details and a snapshot of her driving licence as a rough confirmation of her I.D.

Carla thought it best not to mention how she and her boss argued about wages the week before, knowing how it might look.

The cop texted something, waited, got a reply back, then looked towards Carla. "Detective Bardotsky's wrapping things up, but he wants to interview you in an hour's time. Can you make it to the Johnson Centre station by then?"

Carla nodded. "Provided I can find parking."

As she walked back to her Nova she saw her four co-workers – Marianne, Jay, Marcus and Emily sitting at a window table in *Cliff's Coffee & Cake*. She stopped to wave, then decided to go in.

Em was the first. "Have you heard what's happened to poe-faced Poe? She's been murdered!"

Not to be upstaged, Marcus jumped into the conversation. "I was talking to one of the officers standing guard on the diner's front door. He told me that she'd been decapitated. Her head had been completely cut off!"

Em upped her game. "I heard it had been chewed off. She slipped on a grease spot, went down, and the roaches got her. You know how big and nasty they are in that diner." She sat back on her chair. "Roaches. Or aliens."

Carla immediately felt dizzy as memories broke through. White flashing lights, a droning insect buzzing noise, and a background smell of –

Jay caught her before she blacked out and fell over.

"Carla!" He turned to the others. "Now see what you've done with all this bullshit." To Carla, he said, "You need to go home, get some sleep. Here," he picked up his manbag, rummaged around in it, then handed her a travel pack of Tylenol. "Go home, get some warm milk, and take two of these."

She smiled at Jay. "Thanks, but I've got to go down town for an interview with some Detective first."

*****

"So, you and Gillian Poe didn't argue the day before her death?" 6ft 3 inch Detective Bardotsky sat across from her in Interview Room 3.

Who the hell told them? Carla wondered. "Well, yes, but that doesn't mean I would've killed her."

"Nobody said you did."

"Then why bring it up?"

"We need to be thorough, Miss Lars."

"If you must know, everyone used to argue with Gillian. For a start she wasn't the easier of people to get along with."

"We were told she was particularly hard on you though; always volunteering you for extra hours at the last minute when you'd otherwise made plans. Or berating you in front of the customers, even when you weren't the one to blame. It's easy to see why you might become resentful."

"I wasn't resentful! Jeezus, I've had worse bosses, and I knew the job wasn't forever. I attend night school."

"Really?" Bardotsky put his arms on the table and leaned in towards her. "You know we'll check up on that."

"Yes, really. Here," she fished out her Student ID from her shoulder bag.

Bardotsky turned it over several times between his fingers. "So, can you tell me where you were around midnight to one o'clock this morning?"

"In bed, asleep." She knew better than to say that she was beginning to think that aliens had abducted her...again, and left her outside, naked...again. What explanation could there be other than extra-terrestrials.

"Your housemate says otherwise. He heard you sneaking into the house at around 6am."

Carla froze. What could she say? The truth would now sound like a lie, and a lie would sound even more like a lie.

She looked down at her hands and mumbled something about having been on a one-nighter with a guy, who she was too drunk to remember the name of, or even the details of what he looked like or where he lived. Even while giving her statement, she realized it sounded made up.

Her lawyer arrived and eventually convinced the police to let her go home, but it was made clear that she shouldn't leave town and that she was the main suspect.

*****

Carla was slumped on the sofa in front of the flatscreen TV when Owen arrived home.

"Really? You're watching a true crime documentary after…"

Her eyes focussed on the screen as actors re-enacted a crime scene where a body was found mutilated.

"Shit, I wasn't paying attention," she tried to explain. "Anyway, why did you tell the police you heard me sneaking back into the house this morning?"

"Because I did." He shrugged.

"Now they've chosen me as the prime suspect," she snapped.

"Don't be silly. I also told them you sneak back in a few times a week. Nobody got murdered on those other nights, just last night."

"Well, they don't see it that way. I had to get a lawyer, and the cops told me I had to stay in town."

"I'm sorry, okay? But it'll be fine. You'll see." Owen wandered off into the kitchen.

Carla heard him switch on the radio, find a station, then singing along to the song – some upbeat dance remix – as pans clanged, then the cupboard door was slammed shut. She ground her teeth together. How could Owen be so flippant about this? How could he be cooking dinner and singing along to the radio so cheerfully when he may have ruined her life? Thinking back on it, Owen hadn't been her automatic first choice for a housemate. She'd needed someone who could put two months' rent up front. Being in jail would make her covering half the rent more than a little difficult.

She imagined Owen getting evicted, possessions dumped on the sidewalk and regretting his part in her false incarceration.

"Then you'll be sorry," she muttered.

From the doorway she heard Owen ask, "Did you want dinner? I'm making scrambled eggs on toast."

Carla shook her head. At that moment, the only thing she wanted scrambled was him.

Later she walked quietly into the kitchen and picked up the wine bottle. Just enough for a nightcap before bed. She twisted the screw cap and poured herself a generous glass.

*****

The following morning, Carla woke up on the grass and shrubland about a mile from her condo, stark naked, again.

Although it wasn't the first time, it left her disorientated. The abductions didn't usually happen two days in a row. The discovery of her murdered boss the previous day had caused her to forget her planned internet search for a UFO group to help her.

She began the familiar run of shame back home, ducking behind trees and walls when early morning cars passed by on the nearby roads.

She made it home by 6:20, out of breath and with yet more scratches on her. Being a naked woman in Cherryburge, Brazoria County, Texas, made it difficult to go unnoticed anywhere.

She stood in the dark hallway not bothering to put the light on, catching her breath and looking up towards the bedrooms, listening to the silence. Why wasn't Owen making his usual amount of noise in the bathroom? His bus left the stop at the top of their street at fifteen minutes to 8. Perhaps he'd decided to stay out of her way because he knew he crossed the line the previous day? She concentrated, but still couldn't hear the shower running, or anyone moving around.

She went upstairs, threw on a dressing gown, then tentatively knocked on Owen's bedroom door.

No answer.

She knocked twice more, then had the courage to turn the handle and open the door.

The room was immaculate – *everything in its place and a place for everything* – and the bed hadn't been slept in. So maybe he spent the night somewhere else? It was a bit of a relief him not being there and hearing her come in. One less thing to tell the cops.

It was only after she'd showered, dressed and went downstairs did she finally noticed Owen's shoes in the kitchen doorway. That was strange enough. He was an unrepentant OCD freak and always left them in the shoe rack or by the front door. The scene became stranger after she stepped closer, noticing the shoes were still on his feet. It was as if he was passed out on the kitchen floor. Carla could only see the shoes and part of his legs as she approached. Something told her to turn around, call 911 and let them deal with it, but she couldn't just call them about her housemate acting strange unless…she let out a scream.

Those were Owen's legs, but they were no longer attached to his body. They were severed at the knee. Pools of blood covered parts of the tiled kitchen floor. The rest of his body sat on one of the breakfast chairs. If he had his legs, the sight wouldn't be so harrowing. Owen's facial expression conveyed peace, considering how traumatic his death must have.

Carla closed her eyes to block out the sight. Immediately images came back to her: The lights – white, bright, pulsating – and the mechanical sounds, like metal snakes slithering close by. Owen screaming – the sound like a live recording, playing out right there as an electric chainsaw carved at his legs.

Then suddenly nothing. She couldn't remember what happened next.

"I killed him…." Then she realized she'd said it out loud. How else could she recall his screams and the saw cutting his legs? Why didn't he fight though? Her own skinny and much shorter build should've been no match for Owen. He was a gym buff and had bulked up since stepping up his training regime. She could see no reason why he would be unable to stop her from sawing off his legs.

Instead of calling the police she turned and ran, intending to leave the house, the state and maybe the country. She opened the front door and immediately ran straight into Jay, from the diner. He stood in the doorway, preventing her from stepping out into the front yard.

"Hey, why the rush? The diner's still closed while the police look for evidence."

"Um, I…" Carla had no answer.

"Can I come in?"

"No! I mean, I'm on my way out."

Jay looked at her, then he looked down at her feet. "Without your shoes?"

"Barefoot walking," she responded, sure that she'd heard the words, possibly as some kind of fad in one of Owen's fitness magazines.

Jay squeezed past her and was halfway along the hall towards the kitchen when she caught up with him.

"No, don't…" she pleaded, tugging at his arm, but without enough force to hold him back.

"What the…" he began, stopping short upon seeing Owen's legs. He let out a murmur as he saw the severed legs on the floor and the legless body propped up on the chair.

"It wasn't me. I didn't kill him. I found him like this."

Jay looked at her as he reached out to put his hand on her shoulder. "Right. Don't worry. We need to clean this up and…then we'll move the body before anyone reports him as missing. Was he due to work today?"

"Yes, at the First Mutual bank, in the centre of town," Carla confirmed. She checked the clock on the wall over the dishwasher. "He should've been there about an hour ago."

"So, we don't have much time. Get me a mop and bucket, lots of bleach and…"

"Why are you helping me?"

Jay paused and looked at her with a curious expression. "I've always liked you, and you're in trouble. Now please, get the cleaning stuff. We don't have much time."

She rushed into the hallway to get a mop and bucket from the cupboard under the stairs then, while the bucket was under the faucet running hot water, she got the bottle of Clorox from under the sink and emptied the remains of it into the water.

Between the two of them, they scrubbed the floor until Carla wondered if the large of amounts bleach might start lifting the vinyl floor tiles.

With most of that done, Jay helped her to wrap Owen's body and detached legs in two bed sheets, and used garbage bags to make the whole thing look as less suspicious as possible. That complete, they scrubbed the chair.

Jay sounded exasperated. "It's no good. The blood might've soaked into the joints. We need to get rid of the Goddamn thing. You need to burn it."

Carla felt a touch of relief. There was a garbage can incinerator in the back yard. "Not a problem." She brushed hair away from her forehead. "What will you be doing?"

"Getting rid of the body. If the police come here to re-interview you about Poe, a dead body could look suspicious."

"Right, of course, thanks. Sorry, that makes it sound as if I'm taking this all for granted, but believe me I'm not. I'm grateful for your help. I don't know how I would have handled all this."

"That's what friends are for, right?" His smile seemed kind and reassuring to her.

Carla took the chair outside to the back yard and did her best to break it into burnable pieces. With the legs poking out the top, she doused the contents of the incinerator with barbeque starter fluid and, keeping her distance, she used a long kitchen match to set it alight. As the flames consumed the evidence of her crimes, she wondered whether she had actually killed Gillian Poe. She remembered fuzzy 'scenes – images of Gillian Poe's face coming up close to her own. Then suddenly banishing from her view. And the metallic buzzing sounds in the background.

But then her memories of murdering Owen were equally as hazy too.

When Jay returned, he seemed happy.

As he entered the kitchen she said, "I killed a man and I don't remember any of it, and we just destroyed all the evidence."

"But I helped you, because that's what friends are for."

There was something suspicious about his inappropriate good mood. The way he just happened to turn up at the house, despite never visiting her in the three years they'd worked together.

"Why did you come here this morning?" she asked, edging towards the back door.

The smile on Jay's face dropped. "Aren't you glad I did?"

"Yes. But that doesn't explain…" Carla didn't get to finish her question.

Jay moved to the counter top. "Here, what you need is a glass of red to steady your nerves. Or better still," He took a hipflask from his back pocket, "Something a bit stronger."

He smiled reassuringly as he unscrewed the cap and offered the flask to her. She took it, saying, "I'm sorry." She took a mouthful and swallowed, feeling the alcohol catch at the back of her throat. "It's just that I've been having these problems. Sleeping." She took a longer swig. "And I keep waking up…."

Jay moved towards her. "Naked?"

"Yes…How did you…."

There was a burst of light and her body shook as if having a seizure.

"What?" she managed, before her legs buckled and Jay's arms wrapped around her, the hipflask falling to the floor.

*****

She felt groggy. Looking around, she eventually realised she was lying on the living room sofa, wrists and ankles bound by some kind of masking tape.

From behind her head, Jay said, "You're awake, sorry about this."

Carla twisted her head, but it was awkward to see Jay without twisting uncomfortably. "Did you kill Owen?" she asked.

"He treated you badly."

"You dosed me with something, didn't you? It was in the

Merlot, wasn't it. And the whiskey in the hipflask."

She heard him move closer to the sofa. "Okay, I'm going to explain things to you, but I don't want you freaking out."

"How do you explain all of this?" She waved her taped arms in front of her. Then she felt his breath close to her forehead and started to struggle, moving herself as much as she could in order to escape his touch.

"I love you," he told her. "I wanted to show you how much – that I was prepared to kill for your happiness. I've been watching you for some time now. Years. The way that bitch Poe was treating you? That was when I decided I would stand up for you."

"By drugging me? And the lights? The noise? Then dumping me naked in the middle of nowhere?" She was about to start shouting at him, but he cut her off.

"I thought it might all be a little too much for you to take in at once. So I compromised. I put a mixture of Rohypnol and Phenobarbital in your red wine – the Merlot in the kitchen." He moved closer to her side. She wondered if he'd let himself get close enough for her to punch him in the balls, then she'd try and make a dash for the kitchen. There were knives in a wooden thing on the counter.

She could hear Jay chuckling to himself. "You certainly had a bit of a weird time when I was driving you to the Diner. You kept saying that the oncoming car headlights were aliens, out to get you. Alien abduction…" She could hear the amusement in his voice. "That's why I left you out in the open, naked. It put you far away from the crime so there'd be no association. That, and the fact your clothes got all splattered when I started to work with the chainsaw. Then when Owen–"

A knock at the door made Jay take two steps back. "Did you call someone?"

"What?"

"Does anyone else know about Owen?"

"I posted an update on Facebook, naturally, what the fu…" The tape Jay stuck over her mouth cutting off her sarcasm.

"I'll take that as a no," he said, before leaving the room. She could hear his footsteps in the kitchen, then back again to open the front door.

"Why Detective Bardotsky, what a nice surprise! Come on in. I take it you're here to see Carla?"

"Yeah, I've got some follow up questions I need to ask her."

She could hear the Detective come into the hallway, and the sound of the front door being closed behind him.

"She's in the living room, having a nap on the sofa. You go on through while I get us some coffee."

Detective Bardotsky came through the doorway, then caught sight of Jay in the TV screen, fumbling behind him. Still confused, he looked down and saw Carla, bound and gagged on the sofa.

Before he could fully turn round, Jay had stabbed him in the arm with a kitchen knife, then punched him in the back, shoving the Detective forward into the living room, dropping to the floor.

Jay quickly stepped in close and delivered 4 hefty kicks to the Detective's ribs, then one to the back of his head.

Panting, he said, "I'm just going back into the kitchen for your bottle of wine."

She made muffled noises and looked directly at Jay.

He just smiled. "No, don't you start saying you're sorry. You had your chance, just like the others. You're all the same, you know that? You lead me on, make me kill people for you, just so I can protect you, and what thanks do I get? Well, sorry, but I'm going to move on and find someone who really appreciates what I do for them."

He turned back to the door. "Like I said, I'll go and get your wine, you can have a couple of mouthfuls, and that way you won't feel a thing."

As soon as he was out of the living room, Carla started to fight against the tape on her wrists. She tried crossing and re-crossing her hands, pulling and pushing, anything to create some kind of slack that she could work on.

From the kitchen the sound of Jay opening and closing cupboards, and a half muttered, "Where do you keep your wine classes?"

Then the whole of her world exploded into noise as the back door was crashed open. Voices shouting, Jay trying to run back into the living room, only to be yanked back by his shirt collar and dumped on the hallway floor. Above him was a uniformed police officer, gun pointed directly at Jay, shouting, "Stay still, or I will fire!"

Another uniformed officer danced around the two of them and into the living room, going immediately to Detective Bardotsky. Down on one knee, the officer started speaking into his radio mike: "One officer down at this location, requiring immediate medical assistance. ADW – stab wound to arm, plus injuries to chest, neck and head. Second victim appears unharmed at this time. Location secure, perpetrator is in custody. Request backup forensics once medivac complete."

Radio conversation over, he stood up and went over to Carla.

"This will hurt a little." Then he took hold of one end of the tape covering her mouth, and pulled it off.

Carla started sucking in air. "How did you know that something was wrong?"

"We were part of Detective Bardotsky's backup," he paused, then carried on. "We were here to make sure you didn't do anything untoward. If we'd seen you through the window we'd've stopped the Detective until we were ready to go in via the back." He looked down at the body sprawled on the living room floor. Breath and pulse were good, and his suit jacket had helped to take the worst of the stabbing. "The medics should be here shortly."

He pulled a Leatherman from his pocket and unfolded a blade. "Let me get that tape off."

As he worked on her wrists and ankles, she said, "I conspired to cover up a murder. I mean, I thought I was the murderer, but I wasn't. That's still a crime though, right?"

He shrugged. "Not for me to decide. I leave that kind of thing to the DA. She always seems to sort a way out for those who cooperate." From out in the street came the sound of an ambulance and several Police cars, while from through the open front door came the sound of Jay complaining. "This was the fourth one. None of them ever made good on their promises, you know that?"

"So what happened to the other three?" The second officer held up his hand. "Hold on, before you tell me, you have the right to remain silent. Anything you say can and will be used against you in a court of law. You have the right…"

Carla was left reeling from the sudden realisation that despite not being a murderer, she was the type of person who would cover up a murder to save herself.

Nothing could make that right but owning up to what she had done might be a start.

The Hand That Feeds
Kelly Lewis

"There you go Mrs Collins, three bags of Fresh Frozen. Now, lemme see, two pounds a bag, that comes to six pounds in all."

72 year old diminutive Mrs Collins closed one eye to improve her focus and started to fish around in her purse for £1 coins in amongst the sea of loose change.

Archie Bexford, owner of *Bexford's Pet Emporium*, leaned over the scratched wooden counter top towards her. "Tell you what, love, call it a fiver for cash."

Mrs Collins, who'd never had any intention of ever paying full price when pity always got her a discount, looked up from her rummaging. "That's very kind of you. Thank you. And a big thank you from Winston as well."

Winston was her ancient Alsatian-Doberman cross. His once black and brown snout was now mostly white and grey, and the beast had worse cataracts than she did. That, and the fact it was bloody incontinent. Before he'd finally managed to get her to tie the Devil dog to the round metal bar outside the front window, she would always bring the dog into the shop. Even before she'd got the evil beast completely through the doorway it'd cock its leg and piss on the door frame. Then it would stand in the middle of the shop, twitching, dribbling urine and growling whenever something at its eye level moved or made a noise.

He'd originally had several large wire mesh cages on the floor. They housed guinea pigs, baby rabbits, that sort of thing. He'd kept them low down because they were ideal kiddy magnets. Nothing beats the power of a child who's never heard the word 'No!' Or had its parents give in and purchase the desired creature after throwing a tantrum.

The final straw, in Winston's case, had been a cage of ten chinchillas. Even numbers were good. "You see, they mate for life, so you have to have two, otherwise you're splitting a couple up, and the one left behind will simply pine away." Actually they were worse than rabbits and would habitually jump anything that got too close.

All ten had been pretty active for most of the morning after he'd put their food and water in the cage, and Winston had been attracted to the blurs of fur moving at 90 miles an hour, round and round the cage walls. Archie had gone to the large storage shed out the back, into one of the commercial chest freezers and had pulled out her usual three packs of frozen dog food. Then, on his return, as he'd waited for Mrs Collins to go through the £1 coin routine, he'd watched the dog's curiosity build, to the point where Winston had stuck his nose hard up against the wire squares to get a better smell of the creatures.

Next thing, one of the psychotic grey and white sods stops by Winston's head, sniffs at him, then bites a chunk out of the tip of Winston's nose. The buggers are like any other rodents, they'll chew on anything because their teeth don't stop growing.

Of course, Winston kicks off big time, understandable given the provocation. But with all the barking and snapping, the chinchillas go into overdrive, bouncing off the sides and corners of the cage at around Mach 1. Then *poof!* Three of them blow a ventricle, or a gasket, or whatever, and they're flat on their backs, legs in the air, having bloody heart attacks.

Well, what with the overheads, Winston had completely wiped out any hope of a profit margin.

That was when he'd decided to ban the dog from coming into the shop.

In front of him Mrs Collins made a show of dropping coins onto the counter top and waiting until Archie had counted them up and put them in the till. As Archie had told her after the last 'incident', "Once bitten, twice shy, and we don't want you making the same mistake again, do we?" Euros, Canadian 5 cents, Iranian rials – nothing was sacred, or legal tender, when it came to her inventiveness at trying to short change him.

Satisfied, he scooped up the coins and watched as she'd collected her walking stick and made her way out.

She might be hard work, but she was a loyal and, more importantly, a very regular buying customer.

Archie looked at the hexagonal mahogany and brass case clock on the wall over the boxes bird food and high fibre rabbit pellets. Quarter past nine. The Council waste disposal van would be out the back at midday as usual. If it wasn't for them then he'd be knee-deep in used bedding and animal crap. And Meltons the butchers would be at the back gates around 7pm to offload expired meat and offal – all destined for the Fresh Frozen processing plant – aka the large storage shed at the side of the house. Meltons wasn't the only butcher who saved money by passing their unsellables onto him. All for free, otherwise they'd have to pay to have it properly disposed of. That was why the dog food was only £2 a kilo. He'd spend a little time of an evening trimming and cutting it up, sealing the plastic bags with one of those industrial catering machines. His parents used to pre-cook the stuff in an old 10 gallon bitumen cauldron until the neighbours complained about the smell. After that it was all 'boil-in-the-bag' regardless of how many teeth your dog had left. Mind you, Mrs Collins' Winston could probably still eat the stuff frozen, then go out into the back garden and have a cat for dessert.

He checked the clock again. Time for a mid-morning cuppa and a digestive biscuit or two.

Ten minutes later, sitting in the comfortably worn easy chair in the living room, he looked over at the mantle above the fire place. The fire was a wide three bar electric, which had been bought back in the 1970s when his parents had owned the shop – around the time when the compulsory smokeless zones had been brought in. On the wooden shelf were several photographs of himself and Joanne. One on their wedding day, outside the local church, another of Joanne holding their daughter in the maternity ward. Both were no longer with him. Joanne had succumbed to ovarian cancer fifteen years before, and their little Susie had been the victim of a wife beater of a husband 18 months after that. According to the inquest she'd died instantly. Never felt a thing. Not that that was any consolation.

He dunked a biscuit several times, but when he tried to bring the wet end to his mouth it fell back into his mug.

"Bollocks."

Now he couldn't really enjoy the tea knowing there was a swampy mass at the bottom of the mug. He looked over at the calendar hanging on a picture hook on the wall. Pinned to it by a large bulldog clip was the MoT and service reminder from Pinkerton's the local garage. It was for his old Vivaro van. It had two sliding side doors, plus the back opened as well. It was perfect for transporting cages. He'd have to hose it out before taking it to the garage as the last time they'd refused to have anything to do with it because of the smell. At least the back yard had a manhole cover he could take up to let the water and droppings run straight into the sewer.

Out front the shop door opened, tripping the electric buzzer on the living room wall, breaking his reverie and stirring him into action.

"I'll just be a minute!" Then he took his mug into the back kitchen and put it in the sink. Old 'Butler' sinks were apparently 'trending' and were 'a must have' again. Maybe he should put it on the Antiques Roadshow? It was an original from when the shop had been built in the 1930s and Archie suspected if he dug into the walls he'd find the original gas pipes for the lighting.

Going back through to the shop, he'd been confronted by the twitchy form of Paul Hubbard. His head was sporadically jerking from side to side, and he kept wiping his nose with a rather dubious handkerchief.

"Archie! Arch, my man!" 5ft 7 inches, skinny as a rake, and forever wearing an old olive green parka zip-up. He'd been on methadone for decades, supplementing it with China white now and again, and as was obvious from his eyes, he'd sometimes get a taste for crystal meth.

"What can I do for you Paul?"

"It's more a case of what I can do for you. How much do you reckon these are worth?"

His hands dipped into both side pockets of his parka, came back out again, and deposited two brightly coloured birds onto the counter top. They blinked rapidly, then staggered around rather than walking, as if they were totally confused.

Archie looked up, for once genuinely amazed. "Paul, these are a pair of Lorikeets…."

But before he could ask where they'd come from, Hubbard said, "They'll be alright once they come down."

More mental confusion. "Come down from where?" Archie put a palm against the side of the counter to stop one of the birds from falling off the edge.

"I got this idea, see." Paul carried on regardless. "It was this morning. I'd been having banana toast for breakfast, and sorting out some Jamaican flower tops, separating out stalks and seeds. That's when I remembered."

When he didn't continue, Archie prompted him. "Remembered what?"

"That these birds like mashed bananas. That's what we fed them with last time we went to the petting zoo."

Again the distracted pause, until Archie said, "And?"

"And I thought, if I were to grind up the seeds, mix the powder in with the mashed banana, and then feed it to some of these," He pointed to the two Lorikeets now sitting on the counter in front of them. "They'd get blissed out, and that would make it easier to pick them up and walk off with them."

Archie looked directly at Hubbard. "Are you telling me that these two birds are high?"

Hubbard nodded. "Totally off their faces. Well, off their beaks is probably more correct."

They're not the only ones, Archie thought. "Okay, how much do you want for them?"

"I don't know. Would £40 sound fair?"

"It would be, provided the serial numbers have been removed."

"Serial numbers?"

"Yes, serial numbers. These aren't your average budget Australian budgies or some Chinese knock off peacocks. These are high end merchandise, so they'll have been tattooed accordingly."

Hubbard picked one up, turned it over and started squinting around its tail and between its legs. "How can you tell?"

Archie smacked Hubbard on the head, then took the half drugged bird from him. "I can tell, because I'm a professional, that's how." He picked up the second one and put both of them safely on a nearby shelf. Then, to Hubbard he said, "Okay, as they're still traceable, it'll have to be £20 the pair, best offer."

Hubbard danced from one foot to the other several times. "You couldn't make it £30, could you?" It was clear to Archie as to where the money would end up. The nearest dealer's pocket.

"C'mon Paul. I'm the one taking all the risks here. It's either that, or you take them back to where you nicked them."

Some more foot shuffling, then, "Okay, 20 it is."

Archie opened the till and handed Hubbard the note.

Ten minutes after Hubbard had left, Archie had been on the phone.

"Chedderton Zoo reception, I'm Gillian, how can I help?"

"Gillian, it's Archie Bexford from the Pet Emporium. Is Steph there?"

Moments later another female voice came on the line. "Archie, to what do we owe the pleasure?"

"Well, it's nothing to be alarmed about, but when you come to your evening roll call, you'll find you're two Lorikeets short."

There was something muffled which Archie thought sounded very much like *Shit!* Then Steph said, "I take it someone's tried to sell them to you?"

"'Fraid so. I just paid £70 for the pair. I've got them safe here. If you want to send someone from your security over to collect them?"

"I'll send Jan Denny round with the money. You haven't called the police have you?"

"No. I figured you wouldn't want the publicity if they got involved. Well, not after the Meerkats…. I'll let Jan know who sold them to me. That way you can do your own follow-up investigation. He shouldn't be hard to spot on the CCTV footage."

"Thanks. Jan's about the only one I trust not to try and sell the story to the newspapers."

An hour and two hamster sales later Jan Denny arrived.

Archie smiled at her. "You really do look the part in that uniform."

"Thanks Archie, that's very sweet of you. Now, I understand you have two of our escapees for me to collect."

He went over to the shelves and picked up a pair of cardboard budgie transport boxes. He'd crossed 'Budgie' out and written Lorikeet in thick black felt pen. As he handed them over, Jan passed him an envelope. He took it, saying, "This all seems like some kind of ransom exchange." She laughed as he continued, "The person you want to look out for on the videos is Paul Hubbard. You can't miss him in that grubby parka of his." He let a few moments of silence pass, then asked, "How's your sister?"

There was an awkward expression on Jan's face before she said, "As well as she can be, all things considered. It's not like the brain damage will fix itself." Then she smiled at the boxes in her hands. "On a good day I take her around the enclosures, so she can see the animals. There's plenty of wheelchair access. She loves the parrots when they come down and take food from her. Usually it's hard to tell what her mood is, but in there, with the birds, she really calms down for a while."

"And they still haven't found the driver who hit her?" He knew full well the police hadn't found him – it would've been all over the local papers if they had – but he felt he had to ask all the same.

"No, it seems the bastard is still hiding out somewhere. You'd've thought one of his mates, or his family, would've shopped him by now. Still, I keep hoping someone will find him."

"All we can do is hope." Archie didn't mention that the police had still to bring his daughter's killer husband to justice. Misery may well love company, but there was no point in adding to Jan's. Changing the subject, he asked, "Doing anything this weekend?"

"Not much. Yourself?"

"I'm going to pack the tent and be off down to the coast for the weekend. A little bit of solitude, and some bird watching."

"Sounds like you've got it sorted." She turned to leave and Archie came around the counter and opened the door for her.

At midday the Council refuse lorry came and went, then the afternoon dragged on into the evening, with him shutting the shop at 4.30pm, the usual time for a Friday. By 5.30pm he'd fed and watered the various livestock, and had gone down to *Fry Me to the Moon,* a fish & chip shop two streets across, on the corner of Telford Road. Cod, chips, and a gherkin – the perfect pickle.

With the dinner things washed, dried and packed away, he cleared down the register, leaving enough in the till for Pearl Corrigan to open up with the following morning. He'd already banked the week's takings the previous day, something his father had always insisted on doing.

"That way, if they roll out of the pub pissed on a Friday night, there's bugger all for them to take if they fancy a bit of B and E."

His father had also put around the rumours that he let poisonous snakes loose of a night as well. That might be why the shop had never been burgled.

While he waited for Meltons to drop off the dodgy meat and offal, he'd spread a large tarpaulin out in the back of the van, then added an all-weather rolled up tent, a rucksack filled with several days supplies, and an oversized *Harrod's* green and gold plastic carrier bag he'd taken from the bottom of one of the chest freezers.

Packed and ready for his weekend break he opened the two wooden back gates, then went into the large shed via the side door. He turned on the fluorescent lights and checked down the long walk of shelving that had a mass of bulk goods on them. Dry dog and cat food, for those who didn't want to keep traipsing to the supermarket for sachets and half sized tins. Flea collars, squeaky toys, pet leads and some cuttlefish bones for the budgies. Furthest from the door was the pair of commercial 22 cubic foot chest freezers, occasionally humming to themselves.

At ten to seven the plain white van from Meltons came, offloaded and went, and by 8:30pm he'd cut, weighed and bagged 18 packs – all now resting in one of the freezers. Not all of it was from Meltons. Some of it had been frozen leftovers from previous evenings when the bags had come in under weight. When the pieces were frozen solid it was easier to cut them up with an old bow saw that was always hanging on the shed wall next to the two oval zinc baths. His father used to go out onto the Northfield Common area early on a Saturday morning with a pair of ferrets. He'd usually bring back a couple of still warm dead rabbits that Mum would hang by their back legs from hooks in the shed's rafters. The zinc bath caught the offal when they were gutted and skinned, the waste going down the main sewer under the manhole cover. That's where Archie had learned how to dress a carcass and handle meat without being squeamish. It had also sadly been a long time since he'd had fried rabbit for Sunday lunch.

He looked down at the butcher's block bench and the large knife in his hand.

Susie's husband, Tony Hagen, had been an electrician. Archie had been unhappy about the marriage from the start, but had kept his thoughts to himself. Well, it's what you tended to do back then. He'd also been preoccupied with Joanne's cancer. Trying to keep a brave face even when it was finally diagnosed as terminal. When she was in hospital it wasn't unusual for him to regularly cry himself to sleep.

Then one morning, 18 months after Joanne had passed away, the police had come round.

Susie had been found dead at the bottom of the stairs by her husband, supposedly coming back to the house after an all-night card game. They'd found pills in her stomach and alcohol in her blood. They'd also found bruises "that are inconsistent with a fatal fall, which appear to have happened over an extended period of time." The bastard had been careful not to hit her where it might show. "However," the Coroner had concluded, "I find it impossible to rule this as anything other than a death by misadventure, due to a lack of hard evidence to show both direct physical and mental abuse by Mr Hagen."

Of course now there were laws in place, but not back then.

He'd let things lie for about 5 months – to mid February, when the days were short and the nights still long. There was street lighting to the front of a row of semi-detacheds, but nothing down the side alley and back gate. Plus Tony hadn't even bothered to change the locks, so the spare keys still worked.

He'd parked the van a good dozen or so cars away, then settled down to wait. Just before midnight Tony had come back by taxi – too pissed to drive – and Archie had given the bastard two hours before he'd reversed the Vivaro into the alleyway.

Once through the back kitchen door he'd let his eyes adjust to the low light.

The kitchen was a tip – old food and takeaway packages were on the counter tops – and from the lounge he could hear snoring. Tony, flat out on the couch, his head on top of an armrest. Careful not to make any noise, Archie had reached into the inside pocket of his Burberry jacket, and taken out the small wooden Rounders bat he kept under the shop counter as a deterrent. He swung the bat high, then backhanded it down hard across Tony's throat, smashing his Adam's apple and crushing his windpipe completely. For good measure he'd then put his foot onto Tony's stomach and stabbed the bat down into the damaged larynx.

Tony had died within seconds, and with the added advantage of no blood spatter or trace. And killing Tony had been so enjoyable, so cathartic he'd had to close his eyes and force himself to slow his breathing down to a more normal rate. Didn't runners call it an endorphin rush? An addiction?

He'd then thought about just leaving the bastard's body at the bottom of the stairs, but that was perhaps a bit too obvious, so he decided it was best not to tempt Fate.

Back at the pet shop it had been easy to strip the body, and with a small block & tackle – and a bit of ingenuity – it had been just like dressing a rabbit. The advantage was that you didn't have to skin the carcass.

What could go down the sewer, within reason, went that way, or into the black bags to be collected by the Council. And after several days in one of the freezers Tony was getting mixed in with the rest of the frozen dog food – cut up into 'steaks' and marrowbone pieces. People still took it and cooked it, or fed it to their darlings raw, and he'd been sure that most of his customers who bought the stuff were just squeamish enough not to look at it too closely.

The easiest part of Tony to dispose of had been the head. He'd waited until May, then gone down to Westling on Sea and the old pier. He'd set himself up right at the very end, and spent the day crab fishing before finally cutting the line and letting the picked over head get sucked out to sea on the tide. He'd taken four of the biggest crabs to Jerry at *Fry Me to the Moon,* and Jerry had cooked and cleaned two for himself and two for Archie for free.

It had been about a year before he'd been certain he'd gotten away with it. The police had come round asking questions, but they didn't seem all that energetic at trying to get to the bottom of Tony's disappearance, which had eventually been reported by his family months afterwards.

Every time after that it had become easier and easier, especially after reading the local newspapers.

Archie went back into the kitchen and came out with a bucket of hot water, bleach, and a couple of cloths he kept under the sink. In less than a quarter of an hour everything had been washed and wiped down, and the water flushed away via the downstairs cloakroom toilet.

With everything packed for the weekend, he'd settled himself in the armchair and spent an hour listening to the radio before setting the alarm clock for 4am.

There was nothing he could do for Jan's sister. She'd been consigned to a twilight hell of a near vegetative state when the car had collided with her. Successive heart failures had led to oxygen starvation, which had resulted in her debilitating brain damage.

The bastard hadn't stopped, but had eventually turned himself in to the police two days later. By that time his blood alcohol level was almost non-existent. He'd claimed he'd been traumatised, with the local papers quoting him as saying that it was the shock that had blanked the incident completely from his memory – "like a train driver when someone jumps onto the tracks in front of their train."

Then, while on bail, he'd failed to attend the police station on a daily basis, and they'd been searching for him ever since.

At 5.40am Archie had driven out the back gates, parked in front of the shop, then had gone back and locked up. Pearl had a key to the shop door, and she really did love the animals. Then he'd started driving, heading North up the A1 rather than to the coast, before going cross country until he'd arrived at the Northumberland National Park. No SatNav or mobile phone, he'd trusted to the old way of driving, with an AA map book and a route board. Working his way into the Park, he'd left the van part way up a forestry dirt road, and had carried on, on foot, for several miles, the rucksack on his back and the *Harrord's* bag strapped to the top of it. An hour later he'd found the hiker's wooden shelter as marked on the trail map. It was weather worn but a comfort, giving walkers and backpackers protection from the rain. He rested up for a few minutes before heading back to the Vivaro – leaving behind the carrier bag on the shelter's bench seat.

Driving home, he'd gone down to the outskirts of Scarborough, and had spent a very pleasant night at a coaching inn, the proprietors glad of the out-of-season business, and the fact he paid in cash. "Too much technology can leave you stranded," he'd said to the manager. "You never know when you're likely to find yourself without signals, or defective chip and PIN readers." And you couldn't track cash like you could a credit card or a smart phone.

Back in his living room a day later, Archie settled down into his easy chair with a cup of tea and half a dozen dunking biscuits. He wondered how long it would take before a backpacker, or one of the forestry wardens, would come across the carrier bag with the head and two forearms defrosted in it.

They would obviously notify the police, who would take fingerprints. After 10 months in the freezer, wrapped up in clingfilm, they should be able to pull a good set off the hands. Once they put those on the system then they'd turn up the missing driver, and Jan would finally get some closure for her sister.

Archie sighed and put half of a tea-soaked biscuit into his mouth.

No doubt, come next Friday, Mrs Collins would be back in

and grumble at him, as she usually did.

"Winston really loves to crunch up those little meaty bones you used to sometimes put in those bags. Why don't you put some more of those in for him?"

Why not indeed.

Archie picked up the local newspaper, turned to the Police Updates section and started to read.

The Bodyguard
Paulene Turner

My brief was clear. Keep myself and the woman I was guarding, under the radar. Off the grid. In the dark spaces between the bright city lights.

Am I doing that now, I wonder, as I lift her up, and carry her like a baby in my arms, through a gym studio full of women clapping the 'hero' who saved their zumba classmate?

Did any of them know, I wonder, it was that same hero who'd felled her in the first place during a misplaced merengue manoeuvre? Or in plain terms... Sarah and the zumba class went one way, I went the other. Hard. Onto her foot.

I was meant to be protecting her. Instead, here I am carrying away from carnage of my own making.

"Sorry," I say.

She glares, and shakes her head. "Why the Hell wouldn't you let me show you some of the steps before we came, like I wanted to?"

*****

I'd arrived at her place – a one-bedroom apartment in a small art deco block in Kirribilli, overlooking Sydney harbour – at 7.30 this morning, slipped inside as someone left the building, and found myself outside her door (noting the security was slack).

"Hi there," I beamed when she opened up. "I'm Jackson, from Up Close and Personal Security Service. Are you Sarah Lockhart?"

She scowled as she looked me up and down. Perhaps she didn't warm to my casual vibe – black jeans and T-shirt, with denim jacket, longish brown hair flecked with grey. Or she'd detected on my breath, the splash (or two) of bourbon I liked in my morning coffee. But that wasn't it. Not entirely.

"I don't need a bodyguard," she said. "This is ridiculous."

Slight, sandy-haired and unremarkable in that I-could-be-gorgeous-if-I-tried kind of way, she wore black leggings and a loose grey tank top with *Rock My World* in rainbow shades.

"May I come in?" I asked.

For several long seconds she stood firm, then stepped back with an audible sigh, slamming the door in protest. In my line of work, I was used to this. No-one likes a stranger hanging about peering over their shoulder, judging their activities (and we do judge).

The flat was liveable, but not loveable. IKEA furniture, nothing on the walls. Lots of books though.

"You've been getting death threats," I said, flatly, leading with my Ace. "Is that usual for…" – *what was she meant to be, again?* – "A scientist?"

She tipped her head, like a bird. A pretty, pissed-off bird. "No. It's probably just someone's idea of a joke." She squatted down to tie her trainers.

"So," I said. "Where are we off to?"

She was going to a zumba class at the gym, she told me – whether I liked it or not. Outside of science, this high energy dance class was her one passion. Going was non-negotiable.

I shrugged. "Well, I'm coming with you."

"And what are you going to do, stand at the back of the room, like a nightclub bouncer?"

"Well, not exactly like that. I...err..."

"No. You'll put the others off and only draw attention to me." Her brow puckered. "I suppose you could stand outside and watch through the glass walls."

Gracious of her. *Not.* That wasn't how I worked.

I stretched my cheeks in imitation of a smile. "It's okay. I keep some workout gear in the boot of my car for emergencies such as this. I'll do the class with you."

Now she inspected me a tad more seriously.

"Do you do zumba?"

"No."

"Then can I at least show you a few basic moves before we go? So you don't stand out like a cockroach in a bowl of sugar."

Whoaah! *I've been called a lot of things in my time but cockroach...!* On the plus side, she was smiling now.

"I'll figure it out as I go," I said.

The rest, as they say, is history.

*****

She's quiet on the drive back from class. As we climb the stairs to the first floor, I offer her my arm but she leans on the stair rail instead. Inside, she hobbles across the room and flops down on the sofa.

I get us both a coffee – it's the least I can do – admiring the view of Sydney harbour through the kitchen window as the kettle boils. It's dazzling blue today, sunlight flaring like diamonds on its surface as ferries and yachts cut through the water, past the Sydney Opera House, which looks like a stack of rowboats awaiting a renter.

I hand her the coffee. "We need to elevate your leg." She watches warily as I place her foot onto a cushion, clamping a bag of frozen peas wrapped in a tea towel over the ankle.

"It's not that bad." She goes to stand up. "I need to get on with my work."

"Relax, at least while you have your coffee." I say.

For a moment, she seems about to argue, then she sinks back into the sofa cushions, huffing in irritation. As she blows delicately into her mug, her phone tings. She snaps it up to read a text, her lips twitching into an impish smile. A lover's message, perhaps? I pretend not to notice.

"So a scientist?" I say. "What kind of science?"

"A chemist."

"Chemistry?" I grimace. "My least favourite subject at school. Mr Bertrand, my teacher, did *not* like me. And the feeling was mutual."

"I suppose because of all the clever tricks you did with the Bunsen burner," she says, eyes rolling, unimpressed. So smart-arsery doesn't amuse her? I wonder what does.

"So, are you researching the cure to some terrible disease?" I ask. "Cancer? Greed?"

"No, medicine's not my field," she says. "I study fuel sources."

She's had a breakthrough, she tells me. Early testing is encouraging … results will go to a government committee … for presentation at *The Future of the Planet* conference in Toronto. As I listen, it's like the molecules freeze in the air around me.

By the time she's done, my lips are as dry as the Aussie outback. "So…you've come up with an alternative to petrol? Is that what you're saying?"

"That's the hope. One that's more planet-sustaining."

I put my cup down carefully and walk to the window overlooking the street, standing well back so as not to be seen. Pulling out a folding pair of pocket binoculars, I focus on a van parked across the road. It has *Stern's Electrical* on the side, but I've never seen anyone who looked less like an electrician than the hulk of a guy, with the broken nose, in the driver's seat. His gaze boomerangs to Sarah's window, hand touching his ear as he mutters to himself – or to some kind of partner on a communications device.

"Can you walk?" I ask Sarah.

"Yes, I think so. But–"

"Get your things! Your laptop, phone. Anything to do with the research. We need to go. Now."

"What? Why?"

I help her track down what she needs. She's moving pretty well, if a little slowly.

"Is there a back way out?" I ask.

"No."

"Okay, plan B." I send her to the bedroom to hide.

"What's going on, why do I have to–"

"Just do it. I'll explain later."

She watches as I pull and release the slide of my automatic, her eyes morphing from irritation to dread as she slips under the bed.

I head out the front door, and march purposefully across the street to the guy in the van, thrusting an old police ID through the window. "Officer Caraway, Armed Response," I say. "I'm afraid I'll have to ask you to move on. We've had a report of a crime underway in the area and we'll need this space for police cars, which will be arriving shortly."

"What?"

"Mate, why don't you go to your next job and come back later, after my colleagues and I..." – I raise my arm and wave along the road behind him, as if I see someone approaching "...have dealt with the criminals."

"Fuck!" the guy mumbles, and starts his car. As he drives off down the road, I see his hand touch his ear and lips move. Not long after, a skinny guy hurtles out of the building, jumping into the passenger seat as it slows. They drive off. *Speaking of cockroaches...*

I've bought us time. But not much.

I take the stairs two at a time to Sarah's apartment.

"Quick, time to move!" I say, peering under the bed.

We sneak out of the flat into my car. I put a cap on, as a disguise. *Go Wollongong Lions.*

"Better stay down," I hiss.

"What's going on?" She's hunches below the dash.

"So, well, errr … It looks like the threat made against you wasn't just a random thing," I keep my voice measured. "That was a professional crew going after you."

"After me?" she asks, pink-faced. "Why? Who'd want to hurt me?"

"In my opinion?" *It could be anyone. From a wide range of countries.* "What you're doing will change things. A lot of people don't like change. Especially, not the megabucks they get for oil."

She sits up, her creased brow gradually smoothing as she considers my words. "But, I'm just a researcher. It makes no sense."

We drive to my apartment in Glebe. I figure no-one will look for her there. It's not much to see but at least it's well-stocked with wine and beer. I pour Sarah a glass of sauvignon blanc, from New Zealand – I developed a taste during a trip to the Marlborough vineyards a few years back. As much as I'd like to join her in a glass, I refrain. I need to stay sharp just now.

"I just can't believe this!" She shakes her head, and swallows half her wine in one gulp. "Have you done many of these jobs? Protecting clients from people wanting to … hurt them?"

The question throws me for a moment. I haven't done this kind of serious protection since … the force. *And how did that work out for you?*

"Err, not recently. I usually do low-key stuff." *The lowest.* "Mostly TV people and low ranking celebrities. I stop the paparazzi bothering them. Or corporate types who think they're important enough to need a bit of muscle. Though, usually, there's no real danger."

But for Sarah, the threat is real. She smiles and asks questions about which celebrities I've protected. I give her a few names – some are quite well-known – but she looks blankly at all of them. She's clueless about popular culture.

She picks up her phone and starts texting. Quite soon, a shade of flamingo pink washes through her cheeks. She's speaking to *him*. Or *her*. Aka, *The One*. I place my hand over her screen and lock eyeballs with her. "You can't tell anyone where you are."

"We can trust Alain, my boss." She pulls the phone away, glowering. There's something about the way she says 'boss' that suggests he's more. "I'll just let him know I'm safe."

When she's done, I take the phone and switch it off. "People can track your signal."

She glances around my apartment. There's not much to see. Cheap furniture. Nothing on the walls. Some film mags and books. A bunch of junk mail I haven't thrown away. She and I have the same decorator – Disinterested Minimalist.

I give in to temptation. "Is this guy, Alain, also your boyfriend?" I ask. Given my job here, I figure have some right to know who the main players are.

She swigs her wine. "None of your business. And, it's complicated."

Complicated? "He's married then?"

She doesn't reply, just sucks on the last of her wine and keeps her eyes fixed on the blank walls.

As I pour her a small refill, I say, "Oh come on! You deserve better than that."

"You don't understand."

"I understand lying very well."

"Well, that's not something to be proud of."

Maybe not. But at least I didn't lie about lying.

I persuade her to have a quick shower (despite the lack of a lock on the bathroom door). "Not too much hot water on the ankle, or it will swell!" I call.

While she's in the bathroom, I retrieve her phone, punch in the password (I'm good at reading people's keystrokes upside-down) and scroll through her messages from Alain.

"Miss you, muffin." "My universe is dim without its brightest star?" "Take a photo where you are, so I can picture you."

I check first to make sure she hasn't sent him anything, then type: "Fuck off back to your wife and don't call me again!"

And switch the phone off.

Sarah comes back in, looking refreshed and cool, sits down and rubs her ankle.

"Still a bit tender?" I ask. "Shall I get some more ice?" I always have plenty of that.

"No, it's okay," she says.

"So how did you come to make this scientific discovery?"

As she talks science, her eyes fill with light and a dimple in her cheek appears, hinting at a playful side. I wonder how I didn't see it right off the bat – she's beautiful. And completely unaware of it.

The mood sours when I pop out to top up her glass. She powers her phone back up and checks her messages, discovering a dozen wounded responses from her boss to my messages.

"Did you write this to Alain?" she asks. "How dare you? You're supposed to be protecting me, not ruining my personal life!"

"Trust me, this won't stop him." *Low-lifes like him get keener with a few obstacles thrown in their path.*

"Well, genius," she says. "In one of those messages, Alain says he saw a picture of me on Facebook being carried by some guy through a gym. Some big foot with a big mouth."

Uh-oh. She shows me a post from one of the zumba women. "Hero saves fallen classmate." With a clear picture of our faces. *Not good.* Whoever is after her will know we're together and may be able to track us to here.

"We have to move, again," I say.

We sneak out through the laundry, on the ground floor, then cross the garden bed. I can't spot anyone on the street as we slip into my car. Though, as I change lanes on the main road, I see another vehicle leap-frogging a few cars back.

My phone rings. A picture of Mark, my boss, flashes onto the screen. I answer, driving one handed through the traffic, one eye on the rear-view.

"Hey Jackson, you on the job?" he asks. "Wanna make a little extra? A few people are interested in the location of your client." I look over at Sarah, staring through the window, oblivious. "There's a grand in it for you," he adds.

A grand? Double what I usually get for tipping off the paparazzi about my clients' movements. Then again, the result here won't be just an embarrassing photo on social media.

"Sorry, no can do."

As I go to click off, I hear. "Jack!" I bring the phone up again. "These people are seriously keen to hear from you." Some heavy breathing. "Ten grand."

Ten grand! I know Mark takes a cut. I wonder how much he'll personally make for throwing Sarah to the wolves.

I watch my client. The light from the traffic dances across her face, illuminating tiny lines of worry around her eyes. No doubt she got them from hours hunched over test tubes, fathoming out complex problems to help the planet. All of which will be for nothing if I allow her to be found.

"Can't help you, mate."

"What the fuck!" he says. "Since when are you a hero? Why do you think you were hired for this job? To save the damsel in distress? No, it was so you could give her up, like you usually do. Like you've always done. So why don't you be a good, bad bodyguard and–"

I hang up and switch off.

It's an effort to keep my expression blank, my breathing even. That was tough to hear – that it was my reputation for betraying the people I was meant to protect, that had won me this job. Had I really moved so far over to the debit side of the balance sheet?

I grip the wheel, and press my foot down more firmly on the accelerator. Sarah senses it.

"Jackson? Is everything okay?"

Is it?

"Never better."

I know now what I have to do.

Spotting a small street on the right, I glance in the rear-view mirror then cut across the traffic and swing down it. Then turn right again, into an underground car park. I squeal down several floors, then pull up in a shadowy spot. I bundle Sarah out and get out my smart phone. These days there's an app for everything, including breaking into the car next to us – a blue SUV. Five minutes later I've got the engine purring and we head back out into the traffic again.

"Where are we going?" she asks.

"To the city." *We need to lose ourselves in a crowd. So we can think.*

"I noticed you have a police I.D. in your wallet," she says. "Is it fake?"

I shake my head.

"So you were a police officer? What made you switch to security guard?" There's disappointment in her voice, or maybe it's in the filter through which I hear the question.

My eyes range around the traffic, searching for any vehicle in pursuit. We're okay for now. "I did something I shouldn't have."

She's silent as I explain that I used to work in witness protection. "I was protecting a guy who'd seen a well-known figure commit a crime. When I finished my shift, I had a drink with a police mate of mine. He asked me where the safe house was, where the guy was being kept."

"And you told him?"

I nodded. "I'd known the cop for years." *I thought he was a good friend.* "During the night, the safe house was raided and the witness was killed. The charges against the public figure had to be dropped, due to lack of evidence. And I was discharged from the force."

"Your cop friend was corrupt, and you got the blame?" Sarah summarises it, coolly. I lost my job, which was bad enough. But the guy I was protecting lost so much more. "It wasn't your fault," she says. "Your only mistake was trusting the wrong person."

In my business, knowing who to trust is everything. I'd let him down.

Since then, in my role as security guard, I'd let quite a few others down, too. For a price.

I change lanes, frequently, yet smoothly, so as not to draw unnecessary attention. On the edge of the city we abandon the car – the cops might be looking for it by now – and catch the tram into town. It crawls along the main street, slow as regret.

"So, what I don't understand is why they'd want to hurt me," Sarah says, a crease forming between her brows. "I'm just a researcher. If I die, someone else will just carry on with my work."

"Someone like the married guy you've been texting? Alain?"

She nods, a jaw muscle taut as she clenches. "He's in charge of the project."

The city shops glide by, the Cinema Multiplex, the Queen Victoria Building with its stained glass windows, ever busy with shoppers, as I think this through. With a scientist's logic, Sarah has homed in on an important truth. There's no point coming after her unless it means the project will end when she does. Someone would have to lose the research, discredit her work and get the whole project shelved, permanently. Someone senior to her, who knew all about what she was doing. Okay, so I had a suspect.

"I know you trust Alain," I say. "But will you let me do a little test to put my mind at ease that he's worthy of that trust?"

"Are all security guards as interfering as you?" she asks.

"If they aren't, they're not doing their job."

She folds her arms, lips pert. *Is that how she looks when a science experiment doesn't go the way she thought it would?*

"We'll give him some false information and if he does nothing with it, and nothing bad happens," I say, "I'll be confident he's okay. And you'll have gloating rights."

She presses her lips together so tightly they turn white. She doesn't like it. But as a scientist, she can't deny the logic.

"All right, I'll do it. To prove you wrong."

Over cappuccinos at a grungy cafe in mid-town, we watch video surveillance of my flat on my phone screen. I use Sarah's phone to text Alain: "Here's the address, I'm not supposed to tell you. Kiss." And switch off.

"I never say kiss at the end like that."

"You think he'll suspect something?"

She doesn't reply, just remains sullen as we drink coffee and watch the screen.

Before the froth has settled on our drinks, two men, with necks like bridge supports, break in through my front door, guns brandished. They move from room to room, looking for someone.

One man speaks on a phone. "No-one's here. Yes, I'm sure. We'll wait here for a while, in case they come back."

"That doesn't prove anything," Sarah says. "Whoever made the threat against me might have seen the zumba post online and figured out where you live. You don't know Alain told them anything."

I nod, and don't disagree. She put a lot of effort into coming up with that explanation. A good scientist should explore all possibilities, I know. But they also have to acknowledge the truth, no matter how unpalatable it is. Something about the way she's twisting her lips and gnawing on the inside of her cheek tells me she's doing that privately – even if she won't admit it.

But if it is Alain, if he is the bad apple in the barrel, Sarah's in deep trouble. Who can she turn to, who can she trust? And, more to the point, what's the best way to keep her safe?

"When do you need to deliver the results to this government committee?" I ask.

"In three days' time," she says. "There's a meeting scheduled at the Ministry for Climate Change."

Three days. *She'll never make it.*

"You know what?" I say. "There's no time like the present. Let's deliver the results early, shall we? But we'll do it my way."

Sarah frowns as she considers this, then nods. "Okay," she says. "What's the plan?"

Her sea blue eyes are alert; she's ready to listen to me, and face whatever we have to, together. I feel a twinge of pride at her confidence in me and something else – the strongest desire to be worthy of that trust.

I ask Sarah for the name of her contact at the Ministry of Climate Change. It's the Minister's Political Assistant, Colson Janus. I don't like the sound of him. Not just because it's a hokey name, but because in my experience political assistants often have their own agenda, serving their own interests before anyone else's. I make a note of Colson's name. A bit more googling, and I learn that there's an event at the Opera House tonight. A concert for climate change. The Minister is bound to be there, with Colson by his side, glad-handing the donors and celebrities. And posing for a few media pics. A call to the Minister's personal assistant, an efficient sounding woman of middle years, confirms it.

"So, we're going for drinks at the Opera House," I say.

"We are?"

"But we'll need to dress for the occasion. What's your go-to store in the city, for clothes for fancy affairs?"

"My what?"

I look at Sarah, still in her gym gear, worn at the knees from overuse, and make a wild guess that she doesn't have a go-to upscale boutique.

"We'll just have to explore." I grin.

*****

Drinks are to be served at sunset, overlooking Sydney harbour, so we have a couple of hours to prepare. As a security guard, I go to a lot of swanky functions, so I know the kind of gear we're looking for. When Sarah emerges from the change room in the first shop, in a green cotton dress my grandmother would not be seen dead in, I frown and shake my head.

"We can do better."

She might be a genius at science, but when it comes to glamour, she needs help.

I lead her back onto the street and take her to *Roxanne's*, a designer shop on the first floor of the Strand Arcade with a lot of sequins in the window. My own outfit is easy – black trousers, white dress shirt, bow tie and jacket. But the eponymous Roxanne takes charge of Sarah to find her something appropriate for cocktails with Sydney's glitterati. I sit back on a leather sofa, sipping tea while she tries on dresses in one of three luxurious change rooms.

Emerging in the first dress, her eyes dart about as if terrified someone might see her. *Which is the general idea.* She's a vision in a strapless, silver-sequined dress, shaped, at the bottom, like a mermaid's tail. I can barely tear my eyes away.

"Is this really necessary?" she says, frowning in the mirror.

Not totally. "Oh, yes, absolutely," I say.

"Have you seen how much it is?"

"Just part of the cost of keeping you safe." I've made more, from selling clients out.

"Cherie," says Roxanne, with a broad Aussie accent, "gorgeous! But don't make a decision till you've tried the red."

'The red' is scarlet and dramatic, with feathers among the sequins and a split up the side, almost to the waist.

"Spectacular!" says Roxanne, clapping her hands together.

"No way in the world!" says Sarah, eyebrows tight.

Sigh. "What else you got?" I ask Roxanne.

The next dress is not as showy. It's a rich blue, to her knee, in a sparkly figure-hugging material that somehow accentuates the colour of her eyes. *Perfect.*

"Not bad," I say. I'd like to say more, a lot more, but I sense compliments will only send her back to the changing room to try again.

Roxanne locates shoes and a bag to match for Sarah. I look through the jewellery on display and pick up a chunky necklace with a sun and moon in it. "Appropriate for a climate change concert, don't you think?" I say, trying it round her neck.

"It's pretty," Sarah concedes.

No, you're pretty, I want to say.

I hand over my credit card – aware this might alert anyone tracking us that we're in the city.

We won't have much head start.

*****

As twilight descends, we approach the Sydney Opera House, its sails like egg shells catching the sun's last rays. The Minister's cocktail party is on at the rear, with the full glorious sweep of Sydney harbour on show.

We follow a stream of well-dressed people approaching a security checkpoint. Ahead, someone flashes an embossed invitation at the guard on duty. Just as I thought – drinks, *by invitation only.*

I take Sarah's hand and lead her to the railing by the harbour. We look out at the water, turning golden as the sun slips towards the horizon. The Harbour Bridge stands sentry before us, lights winking as cars whizz back and forth. To anyone observing, we look like any couple having a romantic moment at sunset. I'm slow to release Sarah's hand and tell myself it's to keep up the illusion.

"What now?" Sarah asks. "Do we create a diversion, or pick-pocket the invitation from someone going in?"

I cough out a laugh in surprise. "Well, look at you, Ms *Ocean's Eleven*."

"Ocean's what?" She's genuinely confused.

"Oh, girl. You have spent way too much time in the lab," I say. "One day, someone will have to fill you in on all you missed, while you were burning those bunsens." *Please let it be me.*

A wry smile breaks out on her face, the dimple making a brief appearance, like a glimpse of pirate treasure before the casket lid bangs shut. But when her watery gaze fixes on mine, all playfulness ebbs. "Before I get to things I missed, we have to get through today. So, tell me – Mr Bond – how do you propose we gate crash this soiree of the great and not-so-good?"

I ask her to wait by the entrance. Then head into the Opera House building. I've body-guarded a few celebs at events here and I know where the catering staff work. Putting on my best 'here-to-serve' face, I stride into the kitchen and snatch up a tray of hors d'oeuvres. No-one gives me a second look as I emerge in the middle of the party, offering spring rolls and arancini balls to the sparkling guests.

When my tray is empty, I scan the long drinks table for what I need. A half dozen women's handbags sit on the table unguarded – their owners immersed in conversations nearby. I see one sparkly red bag with The Event invitation spilling out. I grab it, ditch the tray and head for the security entrance.

But Sarah's not where I left her. Panic sluices through me as I consider that someone might have taken her already? My eyes scan the line of people waiting to enter. She's not there. I look further along at the people strolling on Opera House walk – she's not there either. I narrow my eyes to scan the cars cruising along the road nearby, checking she's in none of them.

"Hello." Sarah's in front of me, unharmed and grinning.

"But how did you get in?"

"I told the man on the door I'd left my invite at the office," she says. "I'm not totally helpless, you know."

I chuckle. This is a woman who's competent at anything she turns her mind to, I suspect. Except perhaps interior design. And making the most of her appearance.

I place her arm through mine – we have to continue the charade, after all – and we stride through the crowd, mixing with the glitterati.

For a moment, I imagine how nice it would be if the fantasy were real, if we were simple party-goers attending a concert on Climate Change. Clinging to each other like a life raft in turbulent social seas.

But she's the one here for climate change. Not me. What she's doing could help repair the world. As long as no-one stops her in the next few minutes. And that's where I come in. My job is to mess with anyone who tries to mess with her.

We swipe some champagne and nibbles and look around for our target. It's not hard to spot the Minister for Climate Change – he's surrounded by lobbyists and ingratiaters. His personal assistant, Ruth – a well-dressed, middle aged woman I recognise from Google images – lurks nearby, keeping watch in case he needs rescuing. To the right, I see Colson Janus, the political advisor. Porkier than in his last photo, he quaffs finger food and slugs down free booze as if it's his birthright.

Everyone is in place.

And then I spot ... bridge bollards one and two – the heavies who were at my house earlier – in the queue for the party. Their suits are a size too small, and they look like rent-a-thugs as they scan the crowd with predator's eyes.

"Keep your head down, and go see the assistant now," I instruct Sarah.

From my experience, personal assistants are fiercely loyal with integrity to spare and a finely-tuned bullshit metre. There's usually no love lost between them and 'political' assistants, like Colson, whose breathtaking pragmatism they see for what it is. Sarah needs to trust someone here; I'm hoping Ruth is the one.

I watch Sarah introduce herself. The assistant listens and frowns, not sure at first what to make of the stunning woman before her with the ziplock file. But after a few minutes, the woman's face relaxes into a smile. She's drawn in by Sarah's intelligence and passion for her subject.

Meanwhile, I loiter around Colson, who's scrolling through his phone messages and doesn't notice me over his shoulder. I need to keep him well away from Sarah until her research is safely in the Minister's hands.

The big boofheads are through security now, head-bobbing trying to spot Colson in the crowd would be my guess. I stand between him and them, blocking their view, to buy some time.

I'm keen to know whether Col really is working with Alain.

So I switch Sarah's mobile back on. Half a dozen messages from the guy are waiting, expressing concern that, even from this distance, has a whiff of fakeness to it. "I'm so worried about you." "Tell me where you are, sweetness." "I'll come get you and keep you safe."

I message a reply: "Hi Alain, I'm going home now. But my bodyguard Jackson is delivering our research tonight to the Minister, at a drinks function at the Opera House. Isn't he brave?" *Couldn't resist that last part.* I send a photo of me, smiling with the Opera House behind me. Then switch off, and wait.

I start counting to ten, but only make it to seven before Colson's phone rings.

"He's here? Now?" I hear him say. His snake's eyes slither over the crowd. "Have you got a photo of him by any chance?"

A few seconds later, my mug fills his screen – proof my suspicions were correct and Alain is selling Sarah out. "I'll take care of him," says Colson.

He holds the phone up, comparing the photo with the faces of the men in the crowd. I'm directly behind him and move around as he does, so he doesn't see me right away. I stop when he's almost done a 360 degree turn. He's taken aback to find me, right there in front of him. Smiling.

"Colson Janus, I presume?" I offer my right hand to shake, and as he takes it, I jab him hard in the solar plexus, with my left. "Oof." He doubles over and I hold him down and jostle him away from the crowd. "A few too many hors d'oeuvres, was it, mate!" I say loudly for anyone watching nearby.

We move to the railing overlooking the harbour, where I

deliver a quick sucker punch to his lower back for good measure.

"That's for trying to hurt Sarah."

"Who the fuck are you?" he says.

"I think you know." For a second, his face is a picture. It could be a Google image of Guilt.

"I'll call security," he says.

"Good idea," I say. "And we can explain to them why you have a picture of me on your phone." I snatch his phone while I'm at it. "And how you promised to 'take care of' me. And how your friend, Alain, got some of his friends to go round to my apartment earlier to 'take care of' both Sarah and I."

"I don't know what you're talking about."

"This phone might say differently."

"Give me that!" He leaps for it like a child jumping for a confiscated toy. I pull it away with a parent's relish and, as he lands, I stamp on his foot – hard – in a move I perfected in zumba class earlier.

"Fuuuck!" While he limps around, moaning in pain, I look back at the crowd and see Ruth and Sarah hovering near the Minister, waiting for a chance to interrupt his conversation with some people.

Almost there. I just have to keep Col busy a bit longer...

Unfortunately, the two thugs have spotted us and cross the Opera House concourse with a Terminator eyelock on me. Their thighs are so large, they walk with their feet wide apart, I note.

"Smile!" I snap a picture of them, and quickly send it off to a journo I know.

One of them rushes forward, grabs my phone, and flings it out into the harbour.

"That's littering," I say.

He swings a punch at me. I duck, then kick him in the balls.

His friend, the other bulldog bookend, grabs me from behind, gives me a couple of good poundings on the cheek that make my world spin and a couple of teeth rattle in their sockets. Before I have my bearings again, he lifts me off the ground and starts moving me towards the edge, with his brother bollard wheezing but still managing to block any view of us. I brace my legs on the metal rail and try to push back as I stare down at the dark waters of Sydney harbour, wondering what lies beneath. Fish? Sharks? Discarded rubbish? I really don't want to know.

"I'll be over with the Minister when you're done," Colson mutters.

He might still get there in time to ruin Sarah's introduction. I need to delay him a bit longer.

"There's something you need to know," I shout.

Col crosses his arms and tips his head, dubious. "What." Spitty on the 't'.

"Just a warning," I say. "If you have any more ideas of harming Sarah, I'd think again. Half a dozen lawyers and journos around the city have copies of her research – and instructions to release it with a big song and dance if anything happens to her."

It's true. I sent a copy of her research summary to everyone I could think of before we came out tonight, figuring the more who knew about it, the safer she'd be.

"Fuck!" says Col, pacing and raking his fingers through his hair.

"Time for a dip!" says Apeman number two, lifting me higher, and plonking me down, butt on the railing, with my feet dangling like a kid on a tall chair. I grip the rail with my hands and fingernails, as he exerts pressure. I resist with all I've got, but I won't be able to hold on much longer.

"The journos have your picture too, guys," I say. "As do the people just over there." I incline my head backwards.

The meatheads and Col can't help but turn around. No-one's there, but in that split second, the guy's grip on me eases a smidge. I lean back, grab Col's shirt and launch us both forward.

Over the rail, into the harbour.

I hit the water hard, a full body slap. The shock of the cold makes me gasp. Even six feet under, I'm none the wiser about what's lurking here. It's too dark and murky to see much – and for that I'm truly grateful. Looking up through the water, I see the Opera House, wobbly and ghostly white against the liquorice sky. As I rise to the top, I grab Col's arm and pull him up with me.

We break the surface together, gasping for breath.

"You fucking psycho!" he says.

Half a dozen people have rushed to the edge and peer down at us with O-shaped mouths. Col sinks under again and I drag him back up, putting him in a lifesaver headlock as I tread water, to claps and cheers from the crowd.

"Fuckwit!" Col hisses.

"Smile for the cameras."

A few people take pics – of me grinning and Col coughing up muck – and post them on social media. #OperaHouseHero.

"Are you all right?" someone shouts down.

Sarah's face appears over the railing, full of concern and surprise and then something else – amusement.

"Never better."

A small boat delivers Col and I safely back to Circular Quay where Sarah is waiting.

"You made quite a splash there," she says. She tries to smooth my tangled hair. "You really don't know how to dress for a swanky event, do you?"

There's the dimple, again, not going away this time. I feel heat rising from my neck to my hairline. And I didn't think I could still blush.

"So, tell me," she says. "What did I miss?"

Pay It Forwards
Madeleine McDonald

The public library was the only place Vijay could study in peace, because now he didn't even have his own bedroom. In the intervening three months he'd spent banged up in Rockham Wood Young Offender Institution, his cousin Ashok had arrived for a long stay, and Mum had reorganised everyone's bedrooms in order to accommodate him. Without asking. But there was no point arguing with Mum where family was concerned.

He stared back down at the multi-coloured diagram and frowned. Then for the third time since starting to study, he flicked back to the beginning of the chapter on kinetic energy. Why had he chosen to do AS-level chemistry, when he already had A-level biology under his belt?

Because Mum kept nagging him, that's why.

"You know what the probation officer said, Vijay. You need to catch up on the schooling you missed. One little mistake need not ruin your life. Finish your studies, and you can be a pharmacist, or a doctor even."

Dream on, Mum. Ever since he had done a basic first aid course, Vijay's ambition had been to be a paramedic, riding the streets under a siren and a flashing blue light. Now, of course, achieving that ambition would not be easy, especially since he would have to disclose his record. But he was fed up with shelf-stacking and zero-hours contracts. Good A-level results were the key to applying for on-the-job training, and he couldn't wait to be a part of the front line team.

He had just turned to the next diagram when a middle-aged woman wearing a blue sari under a grey cardigan plumped herself down on the chair opposite, and leaned over the table. "You can help me, yes?"

You what? He did not recognise her, but Mum would give him an earful if he was rude to one of her friends. Who was she and why had Mum sent her to the library? He replied with caution. "Yes, auntie. As you see, I am studying, but what can I do for you?"

"It is my daughter-in-law. I want—" The woman hesitated, and finished in a rush. "I want her removed."

"I don't understand."

"She is bad influence on my son. She has persuaded him to leave home." Her features darkened with fury. "They live in their own flat. They do not give me the key."

Respect! Someone with the balls to stand up to the mafia of Indian mothers. Mum and her friends lived in the past, believing life in England should follow India's traditional customs. In a few years' time, once he finished his training, her matchmaking instincts would kick into gear, and he dreaded the thought of countless tea parties with the sole purpose of introducing him to suitable girls.

The clock said 18.50, and the library would soon close.

Vijay switched off his iPad and collected his notes together. "Auntie, I do not know your family. I do not see how I can help."

"I will pay you £50."

Well, that grabbed his attention.

She lowered her voice even further. "One hundred even. If you insist." She produced a medicine bottle from the folds of her garment and showed him the label.

Vijay whistled. "Hey, that stuff's lethal at the wrong dose."

"Precisely. Take it. Put it in her house. Put it in this." She extracted a larger brown bottle from a plastic supermarket bag and waved it under his nose. "I know she drink this. My son, he tell me so."

His curiosity whetted, Vijay scanned the list of ingredients that went into an all-purpose Ayurvedic herbal tonic, although the smiling baby on the label promised hope. Innocuous stuff, he decided, no different to a multi-vitamin pill in England.

"I do not want her to have my grandson. I want her gone." The venom in her voice sent a shudder down his spine. It reminded him of certain people he had met inside. People he never, ever, wanted to see again.

He stood up, pushing both bottles back across the desk. "No, missus, I ain't getting mixed up in anything like that."

She stood to face him, refusing to back off. "Why not? You are bad boy, I know."

Mum and her gossiping cronies. It seemed the whole community knew about his 'little mistake'. He hoped Mum also bragged about his determination to turn his life around. Studying did his head in at times, but one mistake was not going to hold him back forever.

"But you are also good family boy. You understand my predicament."

Get me out of here! "You're asking the wrong person." He turned to walk away.

She scurried to the door beside him, clutching the supermarket bag. Her hand shot out to grip his arm. Short of physically slapping the hand loose, there was nothing he could do.

"She is bad girl, taking my son away from his family." Her voice dropped to a hiss. "Blood will out. Her grandmother was English."

So what? Plenty of people were in mixed marriages nowadays. He felt sorry for the unknown, part-English daughter-in-law, who didn't deserve such hatred.

A flash of memory, of the prison chaplain droning on, and Vijay came to a decision. He adopted a respectful tone again. "I will walk you home, auntie. The streets are not safe at night."

Listening to the stream of poison the old bat poured into his ears, he recalled the chaplain's words. Along with other inmates, Vijay had attended the weekly sessions 'for all faiths and none' because they offered a break from prison routine. "Pay it forwards. That's important in life," the chaplain often said. "Do a stranger a good turn, and one day a stranger will step in for you."

Vijay walked home with a spring in his step, fingering the medicine bottle in his pocket. One hundred and fifty pounds in new £20 and £10 notes sat in his wallet, because he had talked up the price. Why not? He was going to be the one taking the risk.

Lock-picking was a skill he had learned at the young offenders' institution. He would slip the entire contents of the lethal bottle into something in the old bat's kitchen, and the bride would be free of her interfering mother-in-law. She and her husband might even conceive that baby they wanted.

Pay it forwards and life would smile on him.

Amateur Hour
Claire Leng

It all started with Caroline calling co-worker David's comments on a local Reddit post *full of bull*, saying he was a 12 year-old who has no idea on how to perform a perfect crime. David direct messaged Caroline back in about five minutes with the long message:

KatKitKill25, what I said was from personal experiences. I have done extensive research on the internet, and even without these researches, I can tell you one fact that's common across the likes of Ted Bundy, Jack the Ripper, and Gary Ridgway. Yeah, think about it, think hard about it. I will give you a hint, they are all males. The biology allowed them to keep their calm, think quickly, and strategize their next move. Science said that this level of psychological endurance can never be reached by females because their brains weren't built in the same way as men, they need to preserve the energy for the baby-making. I'm sorry your life is so boring that your poor single mind can't possibly grasp the light that shines into the actual world.

Caroline read the message while sipping her Oat Milk Latte with a smile on her face. She returned the phone to her pocket and switched attention back to her colleagues. Myra and

Stephen were chit-chatting about their holiday plans, while David stared into his phone furiously.

"Cold brew with sweet cream for David." The bartender put down a cup of dark liquid with caramel colored foam on the counter.

David's eyes were still glued to the phone screen.

"David, isn't that your drink?" Carline asked. As if being woken up from a dream, David lifted his head, red-faced, "Oh shit, yes." He tugged a string of his long, dry sandy hair behind his ear, stood up, eyes glued to his phone, messaging while walking to the counter.

"So that meeting was brutal." Stephen said casually, "You two had some nice conversation back there."

Caroline was about to explain herself by starting with an apology, but Myra cut her off, "That was nothing personal, right Caroline? We were just thinking from different angles, that's all. We are all professionals here."

Thanks for womansplaining to me. Caroline thought and smiled, "That's right. I didn't mean to raise my voice at you Myra, but this scope creep was seriously getting under my skin."

Myra shrugged, her perfect dark silky hair bounced around her shoulder, "It's our job to make our clients happy."

"Ha, that's why this one would get a fast-tracked promotion by the end of the year, not you and me," Stephen said and pointed at Caroline and himself.

Caroline's ears started burning. She hoped her colleagues would contribute the flush on her face to the hot beverages.

The phone in her pocket buzzed with another message, but she chose to ignore it.

"I don't know about us, but I know it won't be David," Myra said.

As if on cue, three of them turned and watched David, who was adding more white sugar in his cup.

After a brief moment of awkward silence, Stephen shook his head, "David is a good guy, he just needs to speak out for himself more."

Already bored from the conversation, Caroline went back to her phone and replied to the message:

IDontdoSwamp, thanks for the condescending attitude and nonsense blubbering. That changed my view of how I see the world. Why don't you pat and congratulate yourself, you did it, you did it, you saved the world from mom's basement again. You think I'm a woman from what? From my user name? Gullible boy, do you need me to teach you a lesson or two about not trusting anything on the internet?

I called you out on your bs because there's simply no way that the Royal Oak Crawler slipped into Callaghan's house by the window. If you read the news instead of doing your intensive "internet research" by reading the clickbait titles only, you'd know the windows of that Victorian-style house was locked from the inside, and the only footage captured of the Crawler was seeing him leaving from the garage. Now explain why none of the front door camera, garage camera, nor did the living room camera capture him, CRAWLING INTO the house? I say that he waited besides the garage's blind spot. When Richard Callaghan's car entered the garage, he crouched down, used the car as the cover, and inched into the garage. Then he waited under the car. After people in the house settled, he simply walked through the kitchen where the blind spot was, then he waited behind the stairs, till who knows how long that Betty Callaghan came downstairs to grab water. He strangled her behind the stairs and then waited for another half hour for Richard to come down looking for his wife. Crawler strangled him, too. Then, he pulled the bodies into the kitchen, and stabbed them each thirteen times using the kitchen knife, and left the house through his original route. The garage camera could only capture about half a minute of him walking out the house on foot and disappearing at the corner of the street. That's how it was done. If you don't know, now you do.

*****

That day around 4 pm, while Caroline was checking herself in the restroom mirror, she received another message from David.

Okay man, you talked like you were there. I'm an intelligent man with a successful career and a beautiful wife, blond hair, and blue-eyed. I don't have time to argue with you about how wrong you are. Have a good day.

Which she replied:

All I'm saying is that you don't have "it" to solve the Royal Oak Crawler case, why

don't you stay in your line and let professionals deal with it.

PS: Nice try. I don't believe you have a wife. Maybe you could have a plastic WIFU now that I'd believe.

David replied within thirty minutes:

Fuck you man, you don't know ape-shit. I am on my way to resolve who the Crawler is. Look, this guy only appears around the rich neighborhood in Houston, takes nothing valuable with him. Look at the victims, the Miller Sisters who lived in their trust fund house, Lewie Marshall, a single hotshot lawyer who lived in his townhouse, and then the Callaghan family, who are the owners of the 5 Flamingo steakhouses. Their upper-class status background isn't a coincidence. On the surface, like what any amateur would think, this guy crawled around the neighborhood and killed RICH people at random for fun. We get a case of a semi-patterned serial killer, the only attributes these victims have are rich and well off.

However, I drew the dots on the map. These three households can be as far as 10 miles away from each other, but they are all on the right turn of the east highway I-10. That means you drive on the highway and once you exit; you take the first right turn, the first house you see would be the victim's house. Why did he do that? Easy getaway? Lazy victim picking? If this pattern persists, the next victim's house would move towards the same direction to east I-10, MARK MY WORDS.

And I have a wife, her name is Caroline. We have two beautiful daughters together; they are all blond hair and blue-eyed. But that's not something you UGO would understand.

Caroline put the phone back in her pocket and exited the bathroom. She saw David who was refilling his grey water bottle at the drinking station. Myra walked by carrying an open laptop on one of her arms, another hand typing something. She glanced at Caroline and nodded. Their manager Jeff came by the hall and called out, "Myra, can you come here, fire drill, we need you."

Myra turned with her big charming smile, "On my way boss, that's why I'm here!"

Caroline scoffed, as quiet as she could manage. David had already trudged away.

*****

Two days later, Stephen came by Caroline's cubicle and knocked at her side desk, "Happy hour today at The Social."

"Who else's going?"

"Everyone's invited."

"Then why don't they send the invite on the calendar?" Caroline looked at her email.

"Huh," Stephen pulled his phone out, "I thought they did. Oh yeah, see, Myra sent out the invite," he lowered down his phone and showed it to Caroline. An event named *Let's have some fun!* scheduled from 4 pm - 6 PM booked on his Thursday calendar. "I'll forward it to you." He typed a few times on his phone. "There, you got it."

"Interesting how she conveniently forgot to forward it to me." Caroline turned and looked at Stephen.

"Don't worry about it, she probably just forgot to blast it to everyone, you know how many people we have in our group."

"Seven. We have seven people," Caroline said.

"I wouldn't overthink it; Jeff wants you to be there. You'd love the tapas this place has; they have these brown sugared bacon-wrapped dates…"

So just like every other wannabe hipster restaurant. Caroline thought, looking back at Stephen's expected face. She pointed back at her laptop, "I have a lot to do today, sorry, I really can't go."

"Are you sure?"

"100 percent."

"Well, you lose. I'll send you pictures of the delicious tapas and exceptional cocktails, don't be too jealous."

"Already jealous."

Myra walked by while putting on her jacket, "What are you two still doing here? We're all ready to go."

"Caroline has a lot to do today."

"Yeah, need to play with formulas and generate this report," Caroline said.

Myra frowned, "Aw, let me talk to Jeff, he can wait for that report till tomorrow."

I can talk to him myself. Caroline shook her head, "No, it's fine, I want to finish it myself, too."

"Okay then, see you later, alligator," Myra said and walked away with Stephen.

Caroline sighed, turned back to her world of Tableau.

At about 6:30 pm, someone knocked at her cubicle. It was David, who was holding a steaming mug.

"Oh, David? I thought you left with the group already."

"Nah, I never go to these things. It's meaningless."

"Sometimes I feel the same." Caroline pointed at his mug, "You having a party for yourself?"

"This? Just hot cocoa. Do you want any? I can make you one."

"That's fine."

David took a sip, eyes straight glued to her face. She turned off her laptop, "I should call it a day, anyway."

"Just going straight home huh." David took another sip, eyes traveled down, "You are a good girl, unlike some other people we have."

Caroline heard the light vacuuming sound; Janitors started their cleaning routine early. "Well, I need to stop by my parents' house today, not going home directly."

"That's good." David said, "There's a crazy killer on the loose if you haven't heard."

"The River Oak Crawler?" Caroline frowned, "It's creepy, isn't it?"

"Yes."

"It's bizarre, right? Why isn't this guy stealing anything? Is he just killing for fun?" Caroline put her purse on her shoulder, "Do you think he's a hired hitman or something?"

"That's a new angle. I never thought of it," David said. "Yes, that could explain the randomness. He could've been hired by these three families' common business rivals, but the police always start from searching the suspect from the closest relatives, friends, that's rule number one."

Caroline shrugged, "Just a thought. But without catching this guy alive, we've nothing more than just speculations from the news."

"Yes," David said. He exchanged the mug from his left hand to right hand, and then back the left hand, "You know, Caroline, you are really smart and we share an interest in true crime. I was thinking, if you're free tonight, would you like to grab some dinner with me?"

Caroline tightened her purse strap. David was still standing in the access way out of her cubicle, "Ugh, I'm flattered, David, but no."

David's face reddened, "Got a boyfriend? I've not heard you talk about him at all."

"No. I don't have a boyfriend, but I'm not looking for any dates right now."

"What does that mean?"

"That means, I'm trying to focus on my career."

"No, I meant, what do you mean to say? Why do you people always use career as an excuse?"

"What do you mean 'you people' and 'always'?" Caroline crossed her arms in front of her chest, "David, as I said, I'm flattered but I'm not looking for any relationship. Not to mention that we are colleagues, which would only complicate things. Thanks for your invite, but I need to go, if you could just excuse me?"

Lowering his head, David walked out backward for two steps.

"Thanks," Caroline said and headed down to the elevator.

"Where do you say you live? Be careful of the Royal Oak Crawler." David yelled behind her.

She paced faster without looking back.

That night, at 9 pm, David sent Caroline another DM:

Man, I gave it another thought. I think I've figured it out; I know where this murder will hit next. It will be somewhere near Memorial. You just wait and see.

*****

The next day, Myra was absent from an important process redesign meeting, so Caroline had to step in and present to the clients. Jeff congratulated her after the meeting, "Good job! It was smooth as butter."

The whole morning went through as normal, until they received the email from Jeff again, informing them that Myra had been found dead in her home in a gated community in the Memorial District. The company offered free counselling and employees were free to leave if they felt they needed some time to recover from the shock and to grieve. The email was short and didn't reveal how Myra had died at her own home. Though the rumor had already been raised from the conference room to the garage parking lot, that she was the new victim of the Crawler.

At lunchtime, Caroline's received another DM from "deleted user":

Don't you fucking ignore me. I was right!!

She took in a deep breath and attached all the screen captured conversation to the police hotline email address she'd memorized for the past four months.

By Friday, the COO Parker called Caroline directly, "Caroline, can you please come to my office?"

On the fifteenth floor, the large glass conference room, two uniformed men and a mid-aged woman in DKNY suit sat across the table with Parker and Jeff.

Jeff stood up, "Caroline, there's nothing to worry about. Chief Broussard here just needs to ask you a few questions regarding David and Myra's case."

"I'm here to help," Caroline nodded.

Parker nodded at the mid-aged woman. "This is our corporate lawyer, Michelle. She's only here to advise. You can talk to her if you feel you need any help."

Chief Broussard said, "Caroline, thanks for taking the time to speak with us. This is my partner Detective Anderson." He rose from his chair. "Shall we take this to the private meeting room?"

Caroline bit at her bottom lip as she followed Chief Broussard and his partner into the separate smaller meeting room.

When they were settled, Detective Anderson coughed politely to gain attention. "The reason we wanted to check on you is that David Petterson has confessed that when he broke into Myra Karrel's house, he was under the impression that it was your home, and the anonymous tips we received showed he was...obsessed with you."

Hands flew to her mouth as she murmured, "No…"

"Have you by accident told Mr Petterson your home address? Or Ms Karrel's?" Chief Broussard's soft blue eyes looked at Caroline, his tone encouraging.

"I would never," Caroline said. "David is a bit eccentric, and we don't even talk to each other on a daily basis. He asked me out once but I told him no. I don't think I have given him my address at all."

Broussard and Anderson exchanged a look, then Anderson said, "It seems that he was so frustrated from your rejection, and some heated argument online fueled his anger. It seems he wanted to prove something by...harming you."

Caroline looked thoughtful. "Instead he messed up? He found Myra's place instead of mine? It could have been me he stabbed to death?" Caroline wiped away tears from her eyes, "Poor Myra. She never deserves this."

"Caroline," Chief Broussard hesitated. "We received some anonymous tips about his online activities, and that was how we could make the arrest so quickly. Do you know anything about this anonymous source?"

"No, I know nothing about it. I don't have time to kill on the internet. I don't even have a Facebook account."

The next thirty minutes were routine to check if David had made any inappropriate comments, advances, or had behaved differently around Myra. Caroline just shook her head. "None that I noticed."

"Thank you, that's all. We'll be in touch." Chief Broussard said and shook her hand firmly.

Jeff waited in the large conference room while Parker escorted the officers out. He turned and asked Caroline if she wanted to take the rest of the day off.

"No need, I'm ready to get back to work," Caroline said, her voice still a little thick with emotion.

"Thank God," Jeff said, visibly relieved, "I was worried this might affect you. Caroline, you've been incredibly strong. The month-end is coming up and I'm going to be relying on you to lead the team. I know, this is a lot to ask, but you have been doing a fantastic job supporting Myra, so I don't see why you couldn't step up now she's gone."

"That's what I'm here for." Caroline said.

When she got back to her cubicle, her Team window was packed with inquisitive messages from her colleagues.

Amongst all the "are you okay?" messages, Stephen pinged her, "By the way, congratulations. I heard rumors that with Myra gone, the manager position is yours."

"I don't think we should talk about it yet, since we've just lost two of our colleagues." Caroline typed back.

"Right, that David is such a monster. I always wanted to punch that jerk's face. I knew something was wrong with that dude. Did you notice how weird he was?"

Caroline didn't reply, but a smile slowly creeped on her face.

She logged into her HR records using the admin passwords, updated her address from the Memorial District back to her parent's home address, and went back to work.

Freeing Henry
Joan Hall Hovey

Lila shot up in bed, gasping for breath, Henry's voice following her into waking. The terrible dream still echoed in her small room and inside her head. Henry was calling to her, anguish in his plaintive cry, throat raspy from so much weeping.

When her racing heart slowed, she slipped out of bed, shed the damp flannel nightdress, and stood in front of the vanity mirror. She wasn't muscular in the way a couple of the body-building women at the gym were, but you could easily see the definition of her biceps, triceps, her abdominals. Definitions that didn't show under her usual loose clothing. She gazed approvingly at her reflection, though not out of vanity. Today she felt she was ready.

Yes, it was time.

Henry's voice had grown fainter, though still deep and resonant. Like James Earl Jones. She loved Henry's voice. Though she hadn't missed the accusing note in his railing. She didn't blame him.

"You promised, Lila."

Yes. And she meant to keep that promise. *Such a long time you've waited. Such cruelty you've endured.*

Soon now.

Gathering up what she would need to accomplish her goal, Lila slipped the items into a leather tote bag.

She grabbed her terrycloth robe, padded across the hall to the bathroom. She turned the faucets on full and stepped beneath the shower.

As the weather forecast had predicted, it was a hot and humid Saturday in July. She pulled a blue cotton dress from her closet and skimmed her dark hair into a French roll to stay cool; she would brush it out before she got there. It was crucial that Grandfather not send her away. Not until she'd set Henry free. Her grandfather might well be furious that she would dare to darken his doorway after running away as she had.

The cream-colored Honda was new to her and purred with good health as it took her back to the house where she'd lived with Grandfather until she was fourteen.

Before that, her father had also lived there with them. But he was killed when a truck carrying a load of lumber crashed into his car, leaving it to explode and burn up on the side of the road. A few days after it happened, her grandfather took her to the site. She could still smell the gasoline and boiled paint and rubber. Bits of wood were scattered along the shoulder of the road.

"I'm all you have now, Lila," her grandfather said, taking her hand in his.

As the little car swallowed up the miles of back roads, Lila's thoughts returned to Henry. He'd been her best friend. They shared secrets and laments. Memories flooded, tightening Lila's mouth, bringing a strange expression into her blue eyes.

Catching a glimpse of herself in the rearview mirror, she relaxed her face, her body. She was just worried about Henry, that was all.

Finally, she saw the old sign just ahead on the left: *Ebsen's Mill*. The only remaining evidence of the old mill which had closed down in the early thirties. People moved away; houses were abandoned, torn down. A few summer camps had gone up in their stead, hunting lodges.

She recognized the sway-backed red-roofed barn. Higher up on the hill, the white Baptist church came into view. Soon the car hit the dirt road which ran about three miles. Lila pulled off onto the side of the road, let her hair down and gave it a quick brush.

Too soon she was turning into the familiar driveway.

She exited the car and shut the door, the sound amplified in the stillness. But not all was still. She could hear the murmur of the stream behind the house where frogs croaked and insects whined. She'd swum in that stream as a child which was surprisingly deep in places. Her father was alive then.

She started up the stone walk, near hidden now by tall grasses that appeared to have gone unmowed since her father's passing. Sensing someone watching her, she looked up. The limp curtain on the upstairs window dropped back into place.

He would keep her waiting.

So often a place where you once lived can seem smaller when you see it again through adult eyes. Not so with this house; with its gingerbread trim and long windows, it towered above her. Abram Parson and grandmother Lilias (for whom

Lila was named) had lived here for more than half a century. Abram himself grew up in this house.

Lila came here as a baby, her father had told her. He'd lost his job and times were hard. It was meant to be temporary. Her mother cooked and kept house. Daddy fixed what needed fixing. He lost himself when her mother died of heart failure. Lila had no memory of that time.

Lila was wary of Abram Parson and tried to stay out of his way. Daddy kept promising they would get their own place soon, and it made her happy to think of it, though deep down she didn't believe they would. Daddy was a good man, kind and loving, but he wasn't strong enough for the world. She could always sense Abram's contempt for him and knew that Daddy felt it too. He would slip into the black place in his mind and disappear for days, lose the latest job. She would watch out the window for him.

And then one day he would show up in the doorway beaming a smile at her and it was like the sun had come out from the clouds. He would pick her up in his arms, ruffle her hair and they would both be happy again. He'd always have a little treat for her: a doll, ribbons for her hair, a chocolate bar. If Abram wasn't home, he'd get out the guitar and they'd sing songs. Or she'd place her small feet over his and he'd dance around the room with her and make her laugh.

After the accident, she cried herself to sleep every night. She felt so alone. One night Abram came to her room. 'Our little secret', he said. She was seven.

On another day a woman came to the house and said Lila had to go to school. The school bus would pick her up, which kind of excited her, but Grandfather said there'd be no need; he would drive her to and from school.

A fat drop of rain slid beneath her collar on spider legs as she ascended the wide cement steps. Lifting the brass knocker she brought it against the oak door – and again. The sound reverberated throughout the house.

Soon she heard the slow shuffling footsteps on the old wood floor. They stopped on the other side of the door. A click of the lock and the door opened.

The six years since she'd seen him had bent his back; he carried a cane now. His face was drawn, almost cadaver-like. His milky grey eyes held a smile. Or maybe a sneer. He looked smaller. He had seemed like a giant to her when she was a child.

"I've had a mild stroke," he said, reading her expression.

"Oh. I'm sorry."

"It's okay. I'm fine now." He patted her shoulder, and she resisted shrinking from his touch. "Come in, child. Such a lovely young woman you turned out to be. Of course, you were always a pretty little thing. I wish your grandmother could see you. You favor her, you know. She was a fine figure of a woman, was Lilias. Do you have luggage?"

"I'm not staying long. I have just this one suitcase."

"It's been a long time, Lila. Please, come inside."

Lightning flashed followed by a low rumble of thunder. He looked out at the darkening sky. "I think we're in for a downpour. You don't want your old grandpa catching pneumonia."

Playing on her sympathy, making her feel guilty, ungrateful. Blaming her... she shook the thought away. *I'm here for one reason. To free Henry.*

She smiled. "Very well." At least, he wasn't going to send her away.

"My dear, you must be tired after the long drive."

"No. It's a lovely drive."

"You must have a husband now? Children? Yes?"

"No. I have a job. A nice place to live. No one bothers me."

He nodded, eyes narrowing. "You were young when you left here. But you got on."

"Yes. I found a temporary live-in job as a mother's helper." The woman had broken her arm and needed help with her two little boys. When her arm healed, she helped Lila enroll in the new school.

"I work as a bookkeeper now." She liked working with numbers; she was good at it. She liked the way she could make things come out right in the end.

She looked around. Little had been done to the place. Just as if she had never left. Perhaps an added layer of neglect. This had always been a dark house. Heavy antique furniture, stuffed chairs. Thick musty drapes he kept closed. The heaviness weighed on her even now.

She saw Henry from the corner of her eye but didn't let herself look at him fully. She could sense his joy at seeing her, all anger at her forgotten. Bless him.

His eyes followed her as she left the room. Dear Henry. He had seen her through so much. Cried with her. She with him.

Abram Parson was an avid hunter in his day and had shot the moose. Shot Henry. He was proud of his trophy. It had not been enough to merely take his life, to stand over his dying body, posed with his gun, a prideful grin on his face. In a final act of humiliation, he'd cut off Henry's head and nailed it (though he'd used screws) to the wall.

But Henry was alive and as handsome as ever, even if there was a sadness in his eyes, a weariness that went beyond sadness. But his spirit soared just now. His handsomeness glowed. She glimpsed again the massive head, the magnificent spread of antlers, like open hands, the dark intelligent eyes that, though replaced, embodied his spirit. Some said the moose was an ugly animal. That simply wasn't true; Henry was beautiful. All animals were beautiful in their own way. But Henry most especially.

Lila asked Abram if she might go upstairs and look around. "Nostalgia, I suppose," she smiled.

"Yes, yes," he said eagerly, "you know this house is your home, Lila. For as long as you like. Explore away."

She could tell he was relieved that she wasn't angry with him, hadn't brought a police officer with her. No need for that. Let bygones be bygones. Lila had forgiven him. He was an old man now. Harmless.

Later, she made a supper of potato scallop and biscuits, his favorite, while rain lashed the windows with sudden fury.

"You're still a great little cook." He picked up his mug of tea and slurped it. Her eyes were drawn to the movement of his mouth. She could almost feel it on her little girl's lips, wet, searching, tongue thrusting inside like a venomous snake. *"C'mon, baby, give old Abram a kiss."*

Her eye was drawn to his trembling hand that brought the fork of food to his mouth. The same hand that had slid under the blanket, forced her legs apart while she cried and begged him to stop. Lila flicked the memories away, like turning off a light. No point in harboring old wounds.

She cleared the dishes. Outside the window, the woods were becoming one with the coming night. The rain had eased up.

"I'm glad you enjoyed the meal, Grandfather. Shall we have our tea in the living room?" *Henry would be lonely in there by himself. He'd be wondering. But he'd already proven himself a patient soul.*

"It's good that you're feeling better, Grandfather," Lila said, setting the tray on which she'd placed two mugs of tea, on the rough-hewn coffee table. She poured a little milk into Abram's the way he liked it. Smiled over the rim of her mug. He reached out with his trembling hand and laid it over hers.

She did not move her hand for a moment, then slid it discretely away. The pills that she had ground into powder were already starting to do their job. His eyes were growing heavy. A thread of drool seeped from the corner of his mouth. But she needed to be sure he wouldn't wake up while she freed. Henry understood and waited with her.

Abram's head dropped, suddenly jolting him awake. He rose unsteadily from his chair. "I'm very tired now, Lila so I'm going upstairs to bed. You just make yourself at home."

"I will. Do you need help getting up the stairs?"

"Oh, no. I climb them every night."

He clutched the railing, holding his cane with the other hand, and made his way up to his bedroom like a drunk trying to appear sober. When he disappeared beyond the landing she turned to Henry and smiled. Henry smiled back.

"He'll sleep for a long time," Lila said.

"Did you remember to bring a screwdriver?" Henry asked, in that glorious James Earl Jones voice.

"Of course I did, you silly." She produced it from the tote bag.

Years before, she'd tried to set Henry free, more than once. But she'd always been too small, never strong enough. And she'd been afraid that even if she was successful in getting all the screws out of the board that held him to the wall, she would drop Henry and perhaps break off some part of his handsome rack of antlers: They were seventy inches across, she remembered her grandfather saying. He was proud of his trophy.

Lila felt the power in her arms and shoulders today though and knew it would be fine. With the removal of the last screw, she felt his head beginning to slip in her arms.

"Careful, Lila."

"Don't worry, Henry. I've got you." And then she was easing Henry down off the wall and setting him on the sofa with great care. An enormous sigh escaped him, like the rush of an ocean wave to the shore. "Thank you, dear Lila. Thank you."

"You're welcome."

"You're my best friend, Lila. You've always been there for me."

"I love you, Henry."

A heavy weight came over her then. Never before had she been so tired, so drained in both body and soul, as if someone had attached a hose to her and was siphoning the last drop of energy.

"I'm going to lie down here on the floor, Henry," she said. "I need to rest for just a little while."

She removed the faded patchwork quilt from the back of the sofa, smoothed it out on the floor and curled into a fetal position.

Within seconds, she slept. And in sleep, she dreamed.

*****

When Lila woke, morning light filtered through the drapes, spilling a pale swath of sunlight across the faded rug; dust motes floated in the air. She'd slept straight through the night. Yet it seemed only moments had passed. Somehow it seemed she'd had a terrible dream but couldn't remember the details. Something to do with Henry.

Yes. I saw his antlers climbing the stairs, splashed high in silhouette against the wall. Like black fire. I must have followed him.

She sat up and looked at the sofa where she'd deposited Henry. As she knew he would be, he was gone. The dream returned to her now. And with it her grandfather's scream of terror as the antlers stabbed him again and again, slicing and gouging.

I must have been standing in the doorway, watching. Rise and fall, rise and fall.

Such terrible rage. Even madness. *Henry, Henry, what have you done?*

Lila raced up the stairs, already knowing what she would find.

The old man lay on his back gazing up at her out of unfocused rheumy eyes. Blood trickled from his nose and mouth as he moaned weakly. He seemed to understand it all as his aged body shivered and the final light left his eyes. He stared blankly past the tines of Henry's antlers embedded in his chest.

She switched on a lamp throwing shadows onto the eerie scene and wrapped her arms around Henry's broad neck and pulled. There was the slightest sucking sound as the antlers left his body. The release was sudden and Lila stumbled backward but caught herself before she could fall.

"Thanks," Henry breathed.

"Why did you do...?"

"He deserved it," Henry said simply.

No point in chastising him. No point at all.

She found a rag under the bathroom sink and ran water over it, squeezed out the excess. As she turned to leave the bathroom, she caught her reflection in the mirror; her blue dress was dotted and streaked with blood. She cleaned it with the cold water as best she could. She washed the blood from her face. Her upper arms felt raw and burning. Henry was heavier than she'd thought.

How pale she looked in the mirror. Absently massaging her aching arms and shoulders, a strange calm settled over her. Of course, she was sorry this had happened. A terrible act of vengeance her friend had committed. She had pardoned Grandfather of all sins, long ago.

Back in her grandfather's bedroom, she cleaned the blood from each of the tines of Henry's antlers. Looking into his staring eyes she saw no shred of remorse and could only shake her head in dismay.

"I'll drop you off in the woods on my way home, Henry. You'll be fine. You're free now."

He would roam the woods again the way he was meant to. He'd nibble grass, water-Lilies, munch birch, and willow. Drink cool water from the stream. Unassaulted. Unafraid. She was sure the Lord would allow him that. Henry had suffered so. Surely the Lord would forgive him.

As she had forgiven Abram Parson, her grandfather. Lila was a forgiving soul.

But Henry. Well, Henry knew how to carry a grudge.

The Usual Unusual Suspects

Karen Skinner has always loved reading and has been writing short stories since she was at school. She has always had a particular interest in reading about the darker side of life, but found that a lot of what she was reading didn't have much emotional drama and so started to write for herself.

A member of the *Hertford Writers' Circle* for the last 12 years and regularly contributed to their anthologies, she has just completed her first novel, part of a series. The next instalment is already in progress and due for completion in 2021.

Karen is married and lives in Essex.

Hilary Davidson was a journalist before she turned to the dark side and started writing crime fiction. Her novels include the Lily Moore series—*The Damage Done, The Next One to Fall,* and *Evil in All Its Disguises*—the Shadows of New York series—*One Small Sacrifice* and *Don't Look Down*—and the standalone novels *Blood Always Tells* and *Her Last Breath*. She is also the author of some fifty short stories; a few of the earliest have been gathered in a collection called *The Black Widow Club*. Her fiction has won two Anthony Awards, a Derringer Award, and a host of other accolades. Toronto born and raised, she moved to New York City in October 2001 because of her very persuasive husband, Daniel. She is also the author of eighteen nonfiction books.

Visit Hilary online at www.hilarydavidson.com.

Pauline Gostling has now retired from working at a busy doctor's practice for many years. Since then she has become a successful playwright, having a Murder Mystery play performed at Hylands House in Essex (https://hylandsestate.co.uk/explore/hylands-house/)

In between her husband and Daisy "our mad Jack Russell" she now spends her time enjoying the countryside, and writing short stories.

"Books have always been a great pleasure to me. Walking home from school one day, reading as usual, I walked into a tree. Even this did not deter me!"

By day, **Linda Kerr** is a triple published children's author, under the byline of *Nellie Fearon - https://www.amazon.co.uk/Nellie-Fearon/e/B07NVF69VN –* but at night, she says, she's more than happy to write anything. *I just love scribbling on a page and, if people like to read my stuff, that makes my day.*

Kate Miller is a playwright and journalist who has turned to crime with *Death in the Kingdom of Pines*, her first novel. The story is inspired by her fascination with the 1930s, the golden age of crime fiction, an era of style and of growing crisis in the world. She's combined this with her love for the French Alps – a region she has known since she went to work in Lyon on leaving school (yes, it was a convent school). Kate has an MA in Theatre, a black belt in karate and a useful knowledge of French swear words. She is currently working on the second Marie-Laure novel, The Lake of Mirrors.

www.katemillerwriting.co.uk

Tiffany Lindfield is a social worker by day, trade, and heart, working as an advocate for climate justice, gender equality, and animal welfare. By night, she is a prolific reader of anything decent, and a writer.

Her website at https://www.tiffanylindfield.com/ also showcases her fiction and poetry to great effect.

Lena Ng scuttles around Toronto, Ontario, and is an eight-legged member of the Horror Writers Association. She has curiosities published in over fifty tomes including *Amazing Stories* and the anthology *We Shall Be Monsters*, which was a finalist for the 2019 Prix Aurora Award (Category: Best Related Work). Her 2021 upcoming publications include *The Half That You See*, *Polar Borealis*, *Love Letters to Poe*, *Selene Quarterly*, *The Gallery of Curiosities*, *Green Inferno*, *Dread Imaginings*, *The Quiet Reader*, *Boneyard Soup*, *Death Throes Webzine*, and *Sage Cigarettes*. "Under an Autumn Moon" is her short story collection. She is currently seeking a publisher for her novel, *Darkness Beckons*, a Gothic romance.

Since 2002 **Ginny Swart** has been writing short stories and serials and to date she's had over 800 accepted by anthologies, e-zines, school textbooks and women's magazines all over the world. *Bang on the Money* is her first real foray into Crime fiction, but hopefully not her last.

Ginny is also the short story/creative writing tutor for the online South African Writers College, the New Zealand Writers College and the UK Writers College – and has a collection of 28 of her early pieces gathered under the title *A Patchwork Quilt* (https://www.lulu.com/shop/ginny-swart/a-patchwork-quilt/paperback/product-199594.html?page=1&pageSize=4)

One of these days I'll write the next big novel to come out of Africa!

Sandrine Bergès is a French academic philosopher and Associate Professor in the Dept of Philosophy, Bilkent University, in Turkey. Sandrine has had work published in *The Future Fire, Yellow Mama,* and *Children Churches and Daddies,* and she enjoys writing about Turkey, historical crime fiction, women philosophers, post-apocalyptic worlds and autism parenting.

She can be found at http://www.sandrineberges.com and other places on the Internet.

Michelle Ann King is a speculative fiction writer from Essex, England. Her work has appeared in over one hundred different venues, including *Interzone, Strange Horizons,* and *Orson Scott Card's Intergalactic Medicine Show.* She has published two collections of short stories, available in ebook and paperback from Amazon and other online retailers, and is currently at work on her third. Visit www.transientcactus.co.uk for details.

Amanda Steel is the author of *Ghost of Me*, which was a finalist in the Thriller category of The Author Elite Awards 2020. Amanda has had work broadcast on BBC Radio Manchester and *The NoSleep Podcast*. She also co-hosts a book review podcast, and works as a copywriter. Her personal blog can be found at: https://amandasteelwriter.wordpress.com

Kelly Lewis comes from Devon, likes long walks and cats, detests telephone cold callers, dogs, and certain people who use the expression 'Janner' within her hearing. Her work has appeared in various magazines, including *The Hub, Bottle, 3 x 5* and *Expressions* to name a few.

Paulene Turner is an Australian writer of short stories, novels and short plays. A former journalist, she is currently writing a YA series involving time travel. Her work has appeared in anthologies and publications in Australia and the US. Many of her plays – directed by her - have been performed in Sydney's *Short and Sweet*, the biggest little play festival in the world. She lives in Sydney with her (great sub-editing) husband, twin daughters and twin pugs.

Madeleine McDonald lives on the Yorkshire coast, where the cliffs crumble into the sea, and finds inspiration walking on the beach. Her published work includes radio stories, newspaper columns, Shakespearean sonnets and romance/historical novels. See https://www.amazon.co.uk/Madeleine-McDonald/e/B0044ROIE4

Claire Leng is working as a technology consultant in the United States. English is her second language, and she has been publishing sci-fi shorts in Chinese and English. She has published work on dailyscienfiction.com. When she is not creating new stories, she enjoys reading various genres of fiction, hiking in different countries, and playing video games.

Joan Hall Hovey is a Canadian author, living and writing in Saint John, New Brunswick. Her novels include *And Then He Was Gone, The Deepest Dark*, and *Night Corridor* among others. Available on Amazon and most online bookstores. Her short stories include *Dark Reunion* which appears in *Investigating Women*, published by Simon & Pierre, Canada. To learn more about the author, check out her websites at http://amzn.to/M7mVAR **and** www.joanhallhovey.com